V

D0329038

11/10

DATE DUE

DEMCO, INC. 38-2931

TRAIL'S END

TRAIL'S END

•

Mack Curlee

AVALON BOOKS

NEW YORK

110810

Published by Avalon Books,
an imprint of Thomas Bouregy & Co., Inc.
160 Madison Avenue, New York, NY 10016

Library of Congress Cataloging-in-Publication Data

Curlee, Mack.
　Trail's end / Mack Curlee.
　　p. cm.
　ISBN 978-0-8034-7701-8 (hardcover : acid-free paper)
1. United States marshals—Fiction.　2. Union Pacific
Railroad Company—Fiction.　3. Wyoming—Fiction.
I. Title.
　PS3603.U75T73 2010
　813'.6—dc22

2010018149

PRINTED IN THE UNITED STATES OF AMERICA
ON ACID-FREE PAPER
BY HADDON CRAFTSMEN, BLOOMSBURG, PENNSYLVANIA

Dedicated to the memory of my parents,
Lawrence and Mary, my brother, Edward,
and to the men and women who paid the
ultimate sacrifice for America

Acknowledgments

Thanks to my wife, Elisa, for her patience, encouragement, and belief in me. My children, Tracie and Mark, for their critiques and suggestions. Alan and Patsy Futvoye and Jim Waltman for their interest and encouragement. I would be remiss if I didn't mention John Floyd, a great friend and a fine writer, who encouraged me, gave many suggestions, critiqued my work, and laughed with me and at me in silly moments. His excitement about this project was stimulating. Thanks to all those at Avalon Books who participated in the selection of *Trail's End* for publication. And to my editors, Chelsea Gilmore and Lia Brown, thanks for your expert advice and professional help.

Chapter One

Wyoming, Dakota Territory, 1867

Jed Colter drew up Smoke, the big grulla. After removing his hat, he wiped sweat from his brow. He turned in the saddle, searching the ground for wagon tracks; then his gaze swung around the horizon. The terrain undulated as far as the eye could see. Sparse sagebrush, shortgrass, and prickly pear dotted the prairie. Talus fanned out from the base of a large mesa looming above him.

Duggan, a drifter from Cheyenne, had told Colter of a canyon just beyond a mass of fallen rock and boulders. Like many others who followed the railroad, Duggan picked up whatever small jobs were available. Men like Duggan avoided the law, so why did he volunteer this information?

"I seen a strange-lookin' wagon headin' for the canyon," the nervous Duggan had said. "Looked like a jail on wheels."

Colter doubted Duggan's honesty, but when he saw the immense boulders and clutter of rocks, his curiosity was piqued. Maybe Duggan had been telling the truth. Colter urged his mount forward.

He was running out of ideas. The best he could figure,

the trail led west. The war had ended over two years ago. It seemed only yesterday he had received a letter from his mother stating that his father, Jim Colter, had been taken prisoner in December of '64 by Union forces and taken to Point Lookout Prison Camp in Maryland. One month prior to Robert E. Lee's surrender at Appomattox, Colter received a telegram.

Jed,
    Received information your father has disappeared from Point Lookout. The camp commander does not believe it was an escape. I'm worried. Please come home, Jed.
                                      Your Loving Mother

Colter retraced in his mind every step of his search. Had he missed something? He had looked everywhere and followed every lead. The coal mines of Kentucky and West Virginia yielded little information. Two men had told him of a wagonload of prisoners who were brought in to work in the mines of West Virginia, but they were not allowed near the shackled men or to know anything of their circumstances.

Colter looked for a sign as he cast a wary eye toward the jutting walls of the narrow canyon entrance. The craggy ledges could easily conceal a man. Smoke issued a deep throaty warning and pranced sideways.

"Easy, boy," Colter said as he put a calming hand on the grulla's neck.

Colter reached into a saddlebag and retrieved the field glasses. He surveyed the canyon entrance, but did not detect any movement. He pulled the Colt .44 and cautiously moved forward, swiveling his head from side to side. He saw the blur of something hurtling toward him from a nearby ledge. Colter turned and fired the Colt, but it was too late. He felt the numbing blow to the head, then tumbled to the ground and lost consciousness.

Colter squinted his eyes open into the hot sun. He moved to get up and felt a tug at his throat and wrists. Twisting his head from side to side, Colter concluded he had been attacked by Indians. He lay spread-eagled and secured with wet rawhide thongs between scrub oaks and gnarled pine trees that offered no relief from the penetrating rays of the sun. What concerned him most was the rawhide thong encircling his throat and tied to an oak several feet from the top of his head. When the rawhide began to dry, he would be strangled or his neck would be broken.

Colter looked around and didn't see anyone. The rawhide drew taut around his neck. His breathing became labored. Time was running out. Soon, the Indians would return to check on their prey. He swore at himself for not being more careful.

"I was set up to walk into this trap!" he said, forcing the raspy words through his closing throat.

He had not seen any evidence that a wagon had been within miles of the canyon. Colter drifted in and out of consciousness. He sensed Smoke's presence, but didn't see him. Colter heard the drip of water . . . or was it a dream? He ran his tongue over parched lips that cracked and oozed blood into his mouth. His eyes fluttered open. The merciless sun seared his face and sapped his strength. Colter turned his head and saw a spectral figure seemingly floating toward him from the hazy distance. He closed his eyes and drifted into darkness.

In a lucid moment, Colter again heard the drip of water.

The scuffle of feet suggested his tormentors were back, but something was different. The sun's heat had diminished, and the sound of dripping water was nearer. A rock wall loomed above him. Flexing his fingers, he felt a tingling sensation and realized he was free. He raised up on an elbow and spotted his mount in the distance, watching him. The Henry rifle was still in the saddle scabbard. Why hadn't the Indians taken his rifle? And his horse? Water seeped from the rock wall and coursed its way down and over a lip, then dripped into a cupped-out depression at the base. Colter was startled when he saw what appeared to be the oldest man he had ever seen. The old Indian sat with his legs folded under him. Gray hair cascaded over his shoulders, and the left arm hung useless at his side. The deeply lined face was contorted and drawn to the left.

The Indian stared expressionless at Colter, then nodded. Colter blinked his eyes and wondered if he was dreaming, or maybe the sun was playing tricks on him. He rubbed his wrists and looked down at his bare feet, realizing the Indians had taken his boots. The tingling had left his hands. The old Indian must have cut him loose. But why? What was he doing out here alone? Or was he alone? Colter scanned the canyon. The only other living being was his horse. Scanty vegetation, scrub oak, and pine populated the canyon floor. Colter figured the Indians used the canyon as a staging area for their raids on unsuspecting settlers and the railroad.

He moved over and hunkered before the Indian. The old man's eyes widened and his mouth twitched as he drew back.

"My name is Colter. I—"

A shocked expression blanketed the Indian's face. The old man closed his eyes and slumped forward. Stunned,

Colter found no sign of life in the Indian. There were no markings or anything to indicate his tribe. Colter removed the string of animal teeth from around the Indian's neck.

"Maybe somebody will know what it means."

Colter buried the Indian in a shallow grave at the base of the wall and covered it with rocks. He slaked his thirst from the small pool and splashed water over his face.

With a sense of urgency, Colter found his hat and jammed it on his head. Keeping a watchful eye on the canyon entrance, he caught up with Smoke and stepped into the saddle. Colter pulled the Henry rifle and urged the mount forward. He wondered why his attackers had not taken the grulla. Maybe they tried, but Smoke wouldn't have been an easy catch since he didn't like strangers. The Henry would have been a prized possession, but the grulla would have been better.

Colter drew up at the canyon entrance and searched until he found his Colt .44. After replacing the spent cartridge, he shoved it into the holster and left the canyon. His eyes traversed the horizon as he slipped the Henry into the scabbard. Thoughts of the old Indian haunted him.

Disappointment gnawed at his belly over another failed lead to find his father. Who had set him up? Find Duggan and maybe he would get the answer. Colter was determined to continue the search, but first he needed to get another pair of boots in Cheyenne before going to Lodgepole.

Colter figured Lodgepole had gotten its name because of the abundance of lodgepole pine in the area. The town was cradled in a valley that sloped up the Black Hills where spruce, juniper, pine, and sagebursh mingled. Lodgepole was a gathering of sun-bleached clapboard structures with high false fronts along both sides of a wide dusty street called

Main. The incessant wind, harsh winters, and a withering high plains sun had taken its toll. Huge, red sandstone boulders marked the entrance at the east end of town. The Westerner's Saloon was at one end of Main Street and a church at the other. The good folk demanded it that way. A jail, livery, dry goods store, bank, doctor's office, and Wellsley's Boarding House were the more prominent places of business. It was a dying town.

Lodgepole lay a half-day's ride north of the path of the Union Pacific Railroad. Once, it had been in a direct line with the railroad, until General Grenville Dodge and his engineers found a more suitable route further south.

Colter leaned his back against the front wall of Wellsley's Boarding House. His right hand rested on the butt of his well-conditioned Colt. Like most days in Lodgepole, it was slow, giving him time to ponder his next move to find his father. He squinted in the glare of the sun as he surveyed Main Street from the church to the saloon where drifters wandered in from the plains. Colter ran a finger over the scar under his chin. His face was the color of old leather with high cheekbones, hinting at Indian heritage, perhaps Cherokee. The faded denim pants and dark blue shirt had little room to spare. A black leather vest partially covered the Deputy United States Marshal's badge. Colter was a new breed of lawman the frontier desperately needed. Too often, the one representing the law was on the run and could easily be bought off.

His thoughts turned to Point Lookout. It had been an Army outpost since the war's end. Colter's visit there soon after his father's disappearance had yielded enough information to begin his search. It helped that Lieutenant Daniel Ebetts, second in command at the small outpost, had been a classmate at West Point. His conversation with Ebetts had lifted his spirits.

Colter had asked, "Dan, what do you know about my father's disappearance?"

"We figured they escaped until we received a letter from Mrs. Colter. Along about the same time, one of our men, Sergeant Abe Gibbons, apparently deserted. We've not seen or heard of him since. There were four other prisoners who disappeared along with your father: Jake Lemmon, Matthew Acker, Buck Trendell, and a fellow by the name of Cain. The other prisoners called him 'Raisin.'"

"Describe this Gibbons."

"Big man, six feet, two hundred pounds. Irishman with red hair and face who likes to drink and gamble. And one other thing: his left earlobe is missing."

Then Ebetts had asked, "What have you been doing since you left the Point?"

"I headed straight for Texas. Punched cows on a spread near the Trinity River. Even made a couple of cattle drives east across the Mississippi River to supply the Confederacy with beef. After that, I worked on drives up the Sedalia Trail to Sedalia, Missouri. Then I was a deputy sheriff in Sedalia."

"How did you get to be a lawman?"

"The trail boss liked the way I handled a problem on a drive up to Sedalia. He knew the sheriff there. They needed a deputy, the trail boss recommended me, and I got the job."

"What about the future?"

"After I finish this business, I'm going to settle in the West somewhere. I'm reading law in my spare time. Someday I'll practice."

"Did you ever hear from Easton?"

"The last letter I got was around the time he graduated.

Said he'd met a young lady, and they were to be married. Never mentioned her name. Have you heard from him?"

"No. The last I saw Dave, he was headed for Gettysburg."

Colter had left Ebetts feeling more confident. He had the names of missing prisoners and the description of an Army deserter named Abe Gibbons. Were the prisoners and Gibbons connected? Was his father among the prisoners? It was a beginning.

Chapter Two

The lone rider approaching from the east caught Colter's eye. Aaron Tarbutton, a towheaded boy of six, saw the man coming and ran to meet him. He and the rider arrived simultaneously at Longley's Livery. Asa Longley, the owner, shuffled out to meet them. After an exchange of words, the stranger passed something to Aaron and headed for the Westerner's Saloon. The boy ran toward Colter, clutching a piece of paper in one hand. What would Aaron have this time? Colter's curious eyes followed the freckled boy as he scurried through the door of Wellsley's Boarding House.

Aaron called out, "Miz Wellsley, got something for ya."

"Why, thank you, Aaron."

Colter smiled, shaking his head.

Soon, Aaron emerged, grinning and holding a cookie in one hand and a coin in the other.

"Aaron, who's the gent that rode in?" Colter asked.

"Never saw him before, Marshal." Aaron stuffed the cookie in his mouth and continued in a muffled voice, "Told Mr. Asa he was goin' back to Cheyenne in the mornin'."

"Thanks, Aaron."

The sign over the door of Wellsley's Boarding House squeaked as it swung in the breeze. Colter glanced up and remembered he had promised Ma to get something to stop the squeak.

"Jed?"

Colter turned at the sound of Ma's voice. The smile on her face told him Aaron had brought good news. Martha Wellsley was a handsome, full-figured woman in her late forties with salt-and-pepper hair. A ready smile brought a twinkle to her gray eyes. He figured she was a real looker in her younger years. She and her husband, Caleb, had come west from Baltimore two years before and opened the boarding house. He died a year later of consumption. Her motherly nature had earned her the name "Ma."

"What's got you so lit up, Ma?"

"Jed, Ellen's coming!"

"When?"

"She'll get to Cheyenne tomorrow." Ma wrung her hands and looked up at him expectantly. "Jed, would you meet her in Cheyenne and bring her here?"

"Sure, Ma. You know what time she'll get to Cheyenne?"

She took Colter's hand and squeezed it. "Thank you, Jed. The train will get to the end of track sometime around noon tomorrow."

Passengers to Cheyenne rode the train as far as the end of track, where construction crews were laying track. From there, they were taken by stagecoach to Cheyenne—a four- to five-hour ride.

Colter had seen the picture of Ellen on a table behind the counter. Judging from the photo, Ellen looked like Ma in her younger years. Ma didn't talk much about Ellen, so Colter knew little about her. Lately, though, she had been more wordy about her daughter. He knew Ellen was the only child of the Wellsley's, and she had attended a girl's boarding school in Baltimore. Why would she come out here? Colter had a mental picture of what Ellen would be like and pondered the anticipation he felt.

The Union Pacific train had arrived in Omaha the day before to replenish supplies and add coal and water. After a night's rest, Ellen Wellsley was refreshed and anxious to continue her journey. The red parasol shielded her face from the eastern sun as she waited to board the train that would take her across the Nebraska plains. What if word had not reached her mother? Would there be anyone to meet her in Cheyenne? Annoyed, she dismissed the negative thoughts.

Ellen caught the eye of every man. She was a picture of grace, standing tall and straight. The black-buttoned red blouse and black skirt highlighted raven black hair, topped by a red and black-trimmed jocket hat set at a rakish angle. High cheekbones and a slightly turned-up nose complimented a smile that revealed even white teeth against smooth olive skin. Her slate blue eyes constantly moved, fascinated by the hurried activity around her.

Ellen saw the black-uniformed conductor scurrying about the station. Thick in the middle with a round, flushed face, he fingered a gold watch as he moved among the passengers, attending to their needs.

Ellen stepped forward, and with a slight wave of a hand, said, "Sir."

With a tip of his cap, the conductor replied, "Yes, ma'am."

"Will the train be leaving soon?" Ellen's soft, slight Southern drawl melted the conductor.

Taken with her elegance, he fumbled to put the watch in

a vest pocket and stammered, "We'll be boardin' in ten minutes." He touched the bill of his cap, and continued with a lisp, "The name's Thornton, ma'am, Henry Thornton. I'll be your conductor to the end of track."

"End of track?"

"That's where the construction crews are laying the track."

She smiled. "Thank you, Mr. Thornton. When will we reach the end of track?"

Thornton nervously fingered the gold watch chain. "If we have no trouble and keep on schedule, 'round noon tomorrow."

Ellen's eyes narrowed. "What kind of trouble, Mr. Thornton?"

"Indians."

To evade more questions, he tipped his cap and hurried off.

As her eyes traveled the length of the train, she saw an unusual wagon. Its sides and rear were covered with heavy clothlike material, rolled up enough so that she saw iron bars. Curious, Ellen observed as four shackled men struggled to push the wagon up a ramp onto a flatbed car. A lawman stood a short distance away with a rifle cradled across one arm. Where were these men being taken? The lawman shouted at the men. After the wagon had been secured, the lawman shoved the men into a boxcar and locked the door. Another man joined the lawman and, after a few words, they turned and walked toward her. The lawman, a sturdy and powerful man, had a mop of red hair that matched a face covered with thick stubble. The sleeves of his soiled shirt were rolled up over the elbows, revealing large hairy arms. When he tugged at his left ear, she was startled to see his earlobe was missing.

"Board!" Thornton called out.

Ellen took a seat by a window. Little comfort was found in the wooden seats. A pull-down shade over each window provided relief from the sun. The car was half full when all the passengers were seated. She heard the excited banter of some, apprehension of others. The train lurched forward, its whistle sounding a mournful signal to begin the long journey across the plains.

Ellen wanted today to be a new beginning. The world she was entering was vastly different from the one she had left. That's what she wanted to do, leave it behind. It was time to get on with her life, let go of the past. For three years she had tried to do just that, but the memories of David Easton and what might have been haunted her. The day before their wedding, Easton was instructed to report to Colonel Nathan Oglesby. That was the last time she saw him. Later that day she received a note from Easton informing her he was being sent to Gettysburg. A letter arrived the following week in which he explained what had occurred and said they would be married as soon as he could get time off. She waited, but there were no more letters. Weeks passed, then three months. On a drizzly day, Lieutenant Kilbane came to inform her of David's death at Gettysburg. In her mind, Ellen rejected his death. She had never loved a man as she had loved David and doubted there would ever be another. In her last letter, Ellen's mother had convinced her to come out west, if only for a short time. The change would be good. She could teach the children of Lodgepole and help her mother with the boarding house. Ellen hardly knew where Wyoming was, but her mother was there, and she needed help.

Although she had worked in a Confederate hospital in northern Virginia, Ellen had not taken sides during the war.

She saw wounded and dying and felt compelled to help. The torment etched on young faces lingered in her thoughts and often brought sleepless nights. The news of David's death, she figured, was a mistake. Soon after the war, Ellen visited and helped where she could in Union hospitals, hoping she would learn something of David. Caleb and Martha Wellsley had objected to Ellen's staying behind when they left Baltimore for a new life in the West.

"Ellen, you've got to let David go," a tearful Martha Wellsley had told her.

"Mother, I promise to join you and Father as soon as I finish my work at the hospital. I'll be all right with Uncle Andrew here in Baltimore," she had said.

Martha Wellsley knew there was no changing the mind of her strong-willed daughter.

Ellen provided comfort to men with mangled bodies and spirits. She often cried with them, wrote letters for them, even taught some to read. Ellen shared with them the crinkled photograph of David Easton. One young man in a hospital near Gettysburg had served under Easton, but he was wounded and didn't know of David's death. Her conversation with Dr. Mitchell at Gettysburg had prolonged her search.

Mitchell had looked at Easton's photograph a long moment, then said, "He reminds me a lot of a young man we had in here right after the battle at Gettysburg. Same face, much as I could tell. His right eye was gone and part of his face. For some reason, I remember him. According to his papers, his name was Henry Jackson. We did what we could for him, but as soon as he got on his feet, he left."

Mitchell had shown Ellen what papers he had on Jackson, but none indicated his home.

Time passed, and Ellen accepted that Henry Jackson was

just a coincidence. She finished her work as, slowly, the men were released from the hospital and returned to their homes. Thoughts of Easton and the many other men who didn't return home continued to occupy her mind. A brief relationship with a man in Baltimore brought a fleeting hope of love, but then it died as quickly as it had appeared. She knew it was time to move on.

"Hello, ma'am, I'm Harley Banes," a gruff voice said.

Startled, Ellen looked up to see the man she had seen talking with the lawman.

"Sorry, ma'am, didn't mean to startle ya," Banes said, touching his hat brim. "I'm a construction boss for the Union Pacific."

"Oh, I was daydreaming," she said with a smile.

Banes took a seat across the aisle. Powerfully built, the sun-bleached eyebrows were prominent on a leathery face weathered by the high plains wind and sun. A smile revealed two front teeth that were askew.

Ellen nodded politely. "I'm Ellen Wellsley, Mr. Banes."

"Where ya headin' to, Miss Wellsley?"

"I'm joining my mother in Lodgepole, Wyoming."

"Lodgepole, huh?" Banes rubbed his jaw. "Miss Wellsley, I'd be glad to take ya there. I'm headin' that way myself."

Ellen avoided Banes' stare and looked out the window. "Oh, no thank you, Mr. Banes. Someone will meet me in Cheyenne."

The terrain seemed to roll and pitch one way and then another, like riding over a sea of patchy grass, scattered sagebrush, and scrubby trees. The distance from one point to another was deceiving.

Suddenly, Ellen thought about the wagon and the men she had seen board the train in Omaha. "Oh, Mr. Banes—"

Banes interrupted and smiled. "Please, call me Harley."

Ellen ignored his attempt to get more familiar. "The wagon those men loaded on the train back in Omaha, what is that all about?"

"They're pris'ners, a bad lot, ever one of 'em. Deputy Sheriff Farnsworth is takin' them to the end of track to work off some time."

Ellen turned in her seat and faced Banes. "What did those men do?"

He squirmed under her steady gaze. "I don't rightly know. They bring all kinds. Thieves, murderers, and jes' plain no-good drunks."

Intuition told her Banes was lying. Ellen feigned a yawn. "If you will excuse me, Mr. Banes, I think I'll rest a bit."

"Ya let me know if I can be of service, Miss Wellsley."

"Thank you, Mr. Banes, I'll do that."

Banes touched his hat brim, arose, and made his way toward the rear of the car. She heard a door open and the loud clickety-clack of the train's wheels as it sped along the ribbons of steel. When the door closed, she breathed a sigh of relief. Ellen didn't like what she saw in Banes.

Chapter Three

Asa Longley, stooped and slight of stature, leaned on a pitchfork, resting from his morning chores. A slouch hat covered thinning hair and a face lined by years on the open range. Short on words, he never talked of his past, but he told Colter of his bronc busting days down on the Brazos. Home was a small room with a cot and a potbellied stove in the rear of the livery.

LONGLEY'S LIVERY was whitewash painted above the entrance. Horses nibbled hay in three of the seven stalls. Harness and rope hung from pegs in support posts, and saddles were draped over the stall partitions. Riding gear in need of repair and grain for the animals were stored in a tack room adjacent to the last stall. A buckboard hugged the wall near the entrance.

Longley looked up as Jed Colter approached. By the length of Colter's stride, he figured it wasn't a social visit. Longley looked over his shoulder and said, "Smoke, Jed's comin'."

Smoke tossed his head when he spotted Colter. The grulla stamped his front feet and nickered.

"Howdy, Asa. How's the leg today?"

"Oh, a bit stiff, but it don't hurt none."

Colter reached inside a pocket, pulled out a lump of sugar, and held it under the grulla's velvet nose. He nibbled and crunched the sugar, then nudged Colter. Jed smiled, remembering the day he broke Smoke to the saddle. The battle had lasted all morning and into the afternoon. At one point Colter almost gave up, thinking the grulla was an outlaw. Some would have called him a killer, but Colter was not the kind to leave anything undone. When it was over, Colter knew that Smoke would never quit on him. The grulla had left a reminder, a deep gash under Colter's chin.

"Where ya off to this time, Jed?" Longley drawled.

"I'm meeting Ma Wellsley's daughter in Cheyenne, then I'll bring her to Lodgepole."

Longley nodded and said, "I grained him good, so he oughta be ready to go."

It occurred to Colter that he and Sheriff Luke Radison would be in Cheyenne. Lodgepole would be easy prey for some drifter.

"Thanks, Asa. The fella who came in yesterday from Cheyenne . . . ever see him before?"

"Nope."

"Anything about him that struck you unusual? Did he say anything?"

Longley spit in the dust and rubbed the week's stubble on his chin. "Nope. Did say he was goin' back to Cheyenne today. Ain't seen him leave, so I guess he's still at the Westerner's Saloon. He's ridin' a dun, and he's got some fancy riggin'."

"Show me his horse and rig."

Longley led the way into the shadows of the livery and stopped where a dun was munching grain. Colter noted the left ear was notched in the shape of a half moon. Longley said, "Told me to hide his rig. Didn't want nobody to see it."

Colter followed as Longley shuffled over to a ladder and climbed to the loft. Asa brushed aside hay concealing a yellow slicker. Under the slicker was a saddle. Longley was right; it was fancy for an ordinary drifter. The pommel was silver-plated. Five silver conchos were evenly spaced down the stirrup leathers, and the cantle was rimmed in silver. Colter searched for a name, but didn't find one. He placed the slicker over the saddle and covered it with hay.

"Did he give a name?" Colter asked.

Longley shook his head. "Nope. He's tall and lanky. Got a face like a horse, big nose, and wide-set, droopy eyes. Didn't like the looks of him."

Colter saddled Smoke, shoved the Henry in the scabbard, then waved to Longley before stepping into the saddle. The grulla, with his long, powerful stride, rapidly covered ground. Colter let him run until he had gotten it out of his system, then settled him into a rhythmic canter. Leaving the rolling foothills among juniper and lodgepole pine, he crossed through an occasional valley and over to the flat plains. Colter respected the Indians' ability to blend into their surroundings. He scanned the ridges and checked every wash and draw for a sign of Indians. He skirted around and below the crestline of each rise.

As the town of Cheyenne came into view, Colter thought of Sheriff Radison and the prisoner he had brought to Cheyenne earlier. Radison knew the country and how to avoid the Indian. Colter dismissed any cause for concern. He left Smoke at Moulder's livery and arranged to have a buckboard for Ellen and her luggage.

Since the Union Pacific first laid track at Omaha in July

of '65, it had made rapid progress across the Nebraska plains. Cheyenne had sprung up out of the ground, or so it seemed. Tents and clapboard buildings had materialized, almost magically, overnight. Just a few weeks before, Cheyenne had been nothing. Now there were masses of people bustling with activity, preparing for the coming of the railroad.

Colter stopped at a large tent with UNION PACIFIC OFFICE emblazoned over the entrance. Leaning into the opening, he asked, "When is the next stage from the end of track due in?"

"'Round four," barked a chubby, balding man peering over glasses.

With a nod of thanks, Colter left the tent and made his way toward the U.S. Marshal's office. A restive feeling settled over him at the thought of the stranger in Lodgepole.

It was noon when the train slowed to a stop at the end of track, leaving a skein of smoke on the eastern horizon. Ellen Wellsley sighed. She had tired of the car's monotonous swaying and endless miles of flat land and scrubby growth.

Ellen stepped from the train into the suffocating heat of the plains sun. Scanning the horizon, she saw a desolate prairie, rolling like sea waves. How could settlers endure such conditions? Mountains loomed in the distant west. Or were they a mirage?

She waited as her luggage was loaded onto the stagecoach and watched curiously as the wagon and prisoners were unloaded. The lawman, Farnsworth, came into view. Another man, short and barrel-chested with powerful arms and thick legs, joined him. He removed the wide-brimmed floppy hat, wiped his forehead with a rag, and adjusted the coiled whip over his right shoulder.

The stage driver yelled, "Load 'er up."

Ellen judged the driver and guard to be in their late fifties. In their younger years, these men had been Army scouts and trappers. Their weathered buckskin shirts hung loosely over sagging shoulders. The guard carried a shotgun and rifle while the driver carried a rifle slung across his shoulder. Both carried a gun on their right hip and a large hunting knife sheathed on the left.

"Folks, I'm Ike Jessup," the lanky one said. "I'll be drivin' this here coach, and that old feller over thar's Pete Ashton. He'll be a keepin' the Injuns off'n us." Jessup cut a squinted eye over at Ashton, then broke into a toothless grin.

The squatty, grizzled Ashton snarled through a tobacco-stained beard hanging down to his chest. "Jessup, yore older'n sagebrush. Why, you wuz a stowaway on Noah's ark." He spat a stream of tobacco juice that landed between Jessup's feet. Ashton ran a hand over his mouth and wiped it across his belly. Unlike the deliberate Jessup, Ashton was fidgety and seemed to always be in motion. Mumbling, he wheeled about, climbed up on the stage, and took his seat. Jessup, still grinning, followed and took the reins.

Ellen checked her luggage, then stepped into the stage along with five other passengers.

"Miss, I'm Charles Singleton, and this is my wife, Abigail."

The accent was obviously British. The Singletons sat across from Ellen. In their early forties, both were plump and fair of skin. Mrs. Singleton, a buxom woman with mousebrown hair, was quiet while her husband talked.

Ellen smiled, extending her hand to Singleton. "I'm Ellen Wellsley, Mr. Singleton. I'm delighted to meet you both. Are you on business or visiting someone?"

Singleton released Ellen's hand with a slight bow,

revealing thinned corn silk hair. "We will be setting up a dry goods store in Cheyenne."

Ellen shifted her gaze to the slender, homely woman sitting to Singleton's right. About fifty, her gray hair was pulled back tightly in a bun, accentuating a large nose. Doe eyes looked about nervously. The lines in her face told a story of hardship.

"I'm Mrs. Odessa Usrey," she blurted.

"Please everybody, call me Ellen. Mrs. Usrey, are you meeting someone in Cheyenne?"

Mrs. Usrey squirmed and wrung her hands. With a slight quiver, she said, "My sister and her husband. He's a barber by trade, and she's a dressmaker. I lost my husband and son in the war. The farm was too much for me to keep up, so I sold it to come out here." She smiled shyly and added, "It's a mighty long way from North Carolina."

There always seemed to be something to remind Ellen of the war and David Easton. She looked at Mrs. Usrey with compassion. "I lost my fiancé, Mrs. Usrey. The war deeply touched us both."

Ellen turned to the couple on her left. They were young, in their twenties, and clung to each other.

"Ma'am, I'm Thaddeus Plummer, and this here's my wife, Mary." Plummer nervously tugged at his bowler hat. He was a rawboned man, but his eyes were full of uncertainty. Mary, lithe with dark hair hanging in ringlets around her face, smiled tentatively.

"Newlyweds?" Ellen asked.

Plummer and his wife blushed and tightened their grip on each other. "Yes, ma'am. We been married two weeks. Left Indiana to get a fresh start out west."

Ellen's smile dimpled her right cheek. "I'm joining my mother in Lodgepole, Wyoming."

They heard the crack of Jessup's whip and a hearty, "Yii! Git up thar, you misfits! Git goin'! Yiii!"

The stagecoach creaked and rocked as the team lunged forward, throwing Ellen back against the seat. Passing a swarm of men, she saw some swing picks while others shoveled dirt and rock into wheelbarrows. She heard the ping as hammers struck spikes and saw men hoist a heavy iron rail and place it on crossties to be secured by men stripped to the waist. Their bodies, burned brown, glistened with sweat.

Another crack of the whip, and then Jessup exhorted the team forward. The stagecoach gathered speed as distance grew from the train. She had felt secure on the train, but as they topped a rise, safety would soon be a memory, no longer an ally.

Dust rolled into the stage like a cloud, soon covering them. The rattle and rumble of the stage discouraged conversation.

Ellen scanned the terrain, recalling Thornton's words about Indians. Her heart raced when she saw them. Three Indians emerged from a draw, hidden from the view of Jessup and Ashton. Their copper bodies melded with their horses. How majestic they were on their painted ponies, and what horsemanship! Ellen casually glanced at the other passengers. Given their tranquility, she knew they were not aware of the imminent danger.

"Injuns!" Ashton yelled. A shot rang out, but the Indians were out of range.

"Everbody that can, git on the floor!" shouted Jessup, applying the whip. The stage surged forward, picking up speed. Horror etched the other passengers' faces. Mrs. Singleton whimpered and buried her head on her husband's chest.

"Does anyone have a gun?" Ellen asked.

Plummer said, "I do, but it's in our luggage."

Ellen would not give up without a fight. She lifted her eyes toward the roof and asked Plummer, "Can you get up there and use one of their guns?"

Mary Plummer clutched her husband. Tears filled her eyes. "No! No, Thaddeus, you can't!"

Plummer said, "But honey, three guns will even the odds."

"No, Thaddeus, I can't let you! I don't want to lose you!"

Ellen empathized with Mary Plummer. She said, "I have an idea."

The Indians remained out of range, riding even with the stage. One left the other two and dropped out of sight. Patiently, they bided their time.

Ellen leaned out the stage door window and shouted, "Mr. Ashton, pass us a gun. We can help."

Had Ashton heard her? There was movement on top. Where was the Indian who had dropped behind the stage? Was it he on the stage? Ellen heard a tapping on the door, and then saw the gun.

Taking the weapon, she heard Ashton's warning, "Be careful. That old Colt's got a hair trigger."

Ellen looked around. "Mr. Plummer, do you know how to use this?"

Plummer said, "Yes, ma'am. Ladies, ya'll git down on the floor, like Mr. Jessup said."

Mary Plummer gasped and covered her face with trembling hands. Mrs. Singleton and Mrs. Usrey were speechless. Singleton eased his wife to the floor, then turned to Mrs. Usrey. "Please, may I assist you?"

She responded in a remarkably calm voice. "No, Mr. Singleton, I'll be all right."

Singleton said to Mrs. Usrey, "When those savages get close, get down on the seat beside me."

Plummer said, "Mary, git down on the floor by Mrs. Singleton." He looked up at Ellen. "Miss Ellen, you git down too."

Ellen said, "I'll be all right. I want to see what's going on."

The two Indians were closing the distance. Their war whoops had been faint; now they were growing louder. Where was the third one?

Ashton yelled, "They're Sioux, Ike!"

"You thievin', murderin' varmits, come and git a dose o' lead!" Ashton shouted.

Jessup drove the team at a furious pace. Ashton flattened himself on top, clutching the Henry in his right hand. One Sioux brave carried a rifle. The other two appeared to have only bows. At close range, the Indian was as deadly with a bow as he was a rifle. Ashton's job was to keep them at a distance.

Fear grabbed Ashton when he saw the Sioux raise his rifle and aim for the horses. If the Indian got the lead horse, they were goners. Ashton brought up the Henry and squeezed off a shot. The Indian's horse broke stride, throwing him off target.

Plummer turned in his seat and saw the third Indian closing in. The brave reached out for the stagecoach, attempting to get on top. Plummer's heart pounded as he swung the Colt outside and hurriedly fired. He missed. The Sioux brave eased up and fell back behind the stage. Plummer figured the Indian would try the other side.

Mrs. Usrey covered her face and leaned down on the seat next to Singleton. The Englishman was frozen, eyes round with fear. Mary Plummer and Mrs. Singleton held each other on the floor.

Jessup saw the rock jutting up from the ground and yelled, "Hang on, Pete!"

The left front wheel struck the rock and splintered, causing the stagecoach to weave erratically. Singleton was thrown on top of Mrs. Usrey. Plummer landed on Mary and Mrs. Singleton while Ellen was tossed to where Plummer had been.

The stagecoach tilted to the left. The passengers screamed as the stage pitched on its side in a billowing of dust. Ellen was thrown savagely against the roof and into darkness.

Chapter Four

At five o'clock Jed Colter entered the Union Pacific tent. Crates and boxes lined the rear of the tent. A desk and filing cabinet were centered in the middle with a table out front. The man behind the table was short and wide of girth.

"Any word yet?" Colter asked.

The man peered annoyingly at Colter over glasses. "No, Marshal," he said with an edge. Then he continued, testily, "The name's Weems. Herman Weems."

Colter frowned. "Mr. Weems, is it unusual for the stage to be this late?"

Weems wiped sweat from his face and tersely said, "Yes, it is, Marshal."

"Thank you, Mr. Weems. I'm going out to see if anything is wrong."

Colter spun on a heel and ducked out the entrance, remembering he had told Radison to hang around until the stage arrived.

"Any word yet, Jed?" a gravelly voice asked.

Colter turned to see Sheriff Luke Radison, a wiry man of

27

slight build. The sun-burnished face was lean and topped by a high-crowned black hat pulled low to the ears. Intense mahogany brown eyes peered steadily from under the wide brim.

Colter said, "Come along. We're going out to see what's happened to the stage."

"They ain't heard nothin' yet?" Radison drawled. He twisted his drooping handlebar mustache and rolled a quirly from one side of his mouth to the other.

Despondently, Colter said, "No."

Radison fell in alongside Colter. Soon, they mounted and turned east along the stage route. Crossing over the hills and dropping down to the flat plains, they scanned in every direction for any sign of the stage. The Sioux, Cheyenne, and the Arapaho were active in the area. He kept his eyes on the horizon as Radison checked out likely Indian hiding places.

The well-being of Ellen Wellsley concerned Colter. He didn't like thinking of what might have happened. How would Ma take it?

"How long since we left Cheyenne, Luke?"

"I'd say two hours."

Topping a rise, they drew up abruptly. A chill crawled up Colter's spine, and a wrenching sickness came to his belly. Where the rise flattened out a stagecoach lay, turned on its side. One horse was down while the others stood lazily in the traces. Luggage and pieces of the stage were left in its wake for a hundred feet or more.

Colter jerked out the Henry, and Radison reached for his Spencer. They took a measured look around, but didn't see anyone. Nudging their mounts to a trot, they kept their eyes peeled for movement. Nearing the coach, they saw the driver and guard. One slumped against the coach, an arrow protruding from his chest. Blood trickled from his mouth and down onto his buckskin shirt. The other lay on the opposite side of the coach, his head angled grotesquely.

Vigilant, Colter slipped out of the saddle and examined the arrow. "Sioux."

Radison climbed nimbly onto the up side of the coach. "Nobody in there."

Colter said, "There were eight to ten horses here."

Radison joined him. "Yeah and three of 'em ain't shod."

Colter glanced at Radison. "Three Sioux. Who are the others?"

Radison rubbed his chin thoughtfully and fingered his mustache. "Maybe soldiers from Fort Russell?"

Colter dropped to a knee and examined the tracks. He followed the shod hoofprints and pointed toward a stand of cottonwoods and willows. "They're headed for that creek."

Radison wiped sweat from his brow and scrutinized the ground. "Jed, take a look at this."

Colter and Radison inspected several boot tracks and three smaller tracks that appeared to be made by a woman's shoe.

Colter said, "Let's follow those tracks."

Rifles rested across their saddles as Colter and Radison moved cautiously toward the cottonwoods. Seeing movement in the willows, they brought up their rifles and stopped when a white flag fluttered in the willows. Waiting in silence, they suspected a trick. A blue-coated figure astride a roan moved out of the willows and approached them. Intently watching him, they moved their mounts forward.

Radison said, "That's Sergeant Bradley Yeager from Fort Russell."

A veteran of Indian skirmishes, Yeager was thick in the chest and sat on his mount proudly.

Yeager's bulldog face smiled as he pulled up and leaned forward. "Sheriff, what are you doin' way out here?"

"Marshal Colter and me rode out to see what happened to the stage."

"Where are the passengers?" asked Colter.

"Howdy, Marshal." Yeager put away the flag as he continued, "They're down by the creek. An Englishman has a broke arm, and the others some bumps and bruises. It could've been a lot worse."

Relieved, Colter asked, "How many?"

"There's six altogether. The Englishman and his wife, then there's a young couple, an older lady, and a young lady."

Colter pressed Yeager. "What happened here, Sergeant?"

"Well, Marshal, me and my men were out on patrol when we saw all this dust over the rise. We rode over to see what the ruckus was all about. There was three Sioux chasin' the stage. I guess the stage hit a rock or hole and busted a wheel. That's when it turned over. We got there as quick as we could, but they'd already killed Ike Jessup, and Pete Ashton was dead too. Both good men. Know'd 'em long as I been here. We chased off the Sioux before they could do any more damage. After we got the passengers on their feet, we took 'em down to the creek to get 'em outta the sun. I sent two of my men back to Fort Russell to let 'em know what happened."

Dusk was gathering when Yeager took them to the camp by Lodgepole Creek. This time of the year, it was a dry, grassy creek bed except for a small pool by a driftwood dam. It provided enough water to clean wounds and remove some of the dust. Yeager had posted guards.

Easing from the saddle, Colter's gaze moved over the camp. He spotted the Englishman holding his right arm. Pain contorted his face as a plump lady comforted him. To their right, a young couple clung to each other. An older woman sat across from them, shivering. Blood had coursed down her face from a cut over the left eye. A young woman attended her.

Colter approached the two women and knelt before them. His eyes examined the younger woman's condition. A bruise on her right cheek cast a darkening shadow.

"Miss Wellsley?" Colter asked.

"Yes."

"I'm Jed Colter from Lodgepole, and that's Luke Radison over there by Sergeant Yeager. Ma, uh, Mrs. Wellsley, asked me to meet you in Cheyenne. Are you all right?"

Fatigued, she said, "Yes, except for some bruises and a headache."

"Excuse me, ma'am."

Colter moved to the center of the group. "Folks, I'm Jed Colter, United States Deputy Marshal, and that's Sheriff Luke Radison from Lodgepole," he said, waving a hand in Radison's direction. "With the help of Sergeant Yeager and his men, we're going to get you safely to Cheyenne as soon as possible."

After a pause, Colter continued. "Sheriff Radison, you go back to Cheyenne and let the Union Pacific know what's happened. See if there's another stage to send out. If not, bring another wheel so we can get this one going. And find somebody to get word to Mrs. Wellsley. I don't care how late it is. Sergeant, have your men put the bodies of the driver and guard on two of the horses from the team so that Sheriff Radison can take them. Have your men gather up the luggage. We need firewood, slickers, and bedrolls. Is anyone else expected in Cheyenne?"

"Mrs. Usrey is to meet her sister," Ellen said.

"What's your sister's name, Mrs. Usrey?" Colter asked.

Weakly, she answered, "Susan York. Her husband's name is Chester."

"Anybody else?"

Getting no response, Colter saw Radison check the cinches and step into the saddle. He grabbed the reins and said, "Hurry, Luke. I don't know how much longer these folks can hold up under these conditions."

Radison nodded. "I'll be back 'round midnight." He nudged his mount and slipped through the willows.

Turning to Yeager, Colter whispered, "Sergeant, have your men check the horse that's down. If its leg is broken, take care of it."

One of Yeager's men dumped an armload of wood in the center of the camp. From a piece of wood, Colter made a splint for the Englishman's arm. His eyes discreetly followed Ellen as she busily helped others.

Colter felt a presence at his side. "Sir, I'm Thaddeus Plummer, and that's my wife, Mary," he said, pointing to a young woman huddled under a slicker. "What can I do?"

Colter, noting the lump over Plummer's right eye, reached into a pocket and withdrew matches. "Start a fire."

Plummer said eagerly, "Yes, sir!"

Colter advised, "Clear out a spot so we don't start a grass fire."

"Yes, sir!"

It was dark when Plummer stepped back, admiring his handiwork. As the flames grew, anxieties diminished.

Colter knelt by the Englishman and his wife. She touched the abrasion on her right cheek. Ellen moved quietly to his side. "Marshal Colter, this is Mr. Charles Singleton and his wife, Abigail."

Even in her disheveled condition, Ellen was as beautiful as he had imagined. Suddenly, Colter's heart pounded.

He tugged at his hat. "Ma'am, I'm sorry we have to meet under these circumstances. Mr. Singleton, how is that arm?"

Singleton winced when he moved. "Hurts like the dickens, Marshal. Thank God you and the others are here."

Colter said, "Let me take a look." He gently moved his fingers over Singleton's arm and knew it would have to be set. It was a clean break between the wrist and elbow.

"Mr. Singleton, I'll have to set your arm, and I'm afraid it's going to hurt."

Singleton looked up at his wife and then at Colter. "Do what you have to do, Marshal."

A shot rang out and reverberated across the plains. Colter heard gasps and saw fear on each face.

Yeager said, "No need for fear, folks. That's one of my men, probably shootin' at a coyote."

Colter found a stick. "Mr. Singleton, put this between your teeth and bite down when the pain hits."

Beads of perspiration formed on Singleton's brow. Mrs. Singleton wiped his face with a damp cloth.

Colter retrieved his bedroll and two rawhide saddle strings. After rolling out the bedroll by the fire, he said, "Mrs. Singleton, we need to move him over here by the fire where his head can rest on my bedroll. Plummer, I want you to put your hands on Mr. Singleton's shoulders and hold him steady."

Plummer's eyes widened. "Yes, sir!"

After Singleton had moved over by the fire, Colter extended the wounded man's arm. Ellen was wiping Singleton's face when Colter looked up. Their eyes met and held for a moment. He saw the slight smile before she looked away. Colter caught himself and wondered if the others had noticed.

Colter snapped, "One of you men get over here and hold down Mr. Singleton's legs!"

Colter's talking distracted Singleton. The Englishman's body went rigid with the sudden burst of pain, and then it was over.

Colter took the stick from Singleton's clenched teeth. "Mr. Singleton, your arm is set. I need to put on a splint, and then we'll be through."

Singleton looked up at Colter and grinned. "It's set? You're good, Marshal! You ever think about becoming a medical doctor?"

Colter replied casually, "It's something we learn to do out here. Does anyone have any whiskey? It might help ease Mr. Singleton's pain."

Colter looked around the circle, but no one acknowledged having any. He figured Yeager's men wouldn't admit it if they did.

Singleton raised his good arm and waved off the effort. "That's quite all right, Marshal. I do not imbibe in hard drink."

When Colter finished with the splint, Singleton smiled. "Thank you, Marshal. It feels somewhat better."

Colter helped Singleton into the bedroll and pulled a blanket up to his chin. Rustling in the willows brought Colter's hand to his .44, but he eased off when he saw it was Yeager's men.

Yeager said, "Marshal, the men gathered up all the luggage they could find and put it back on the stage."

Colter nodded his thanks. "I know you all must be hungry. We have hardtack, some jerked beef, and a few biscuits. We'll make some coffee."

"I'll have some, Marshal," Thaddeus Plummer said.

The others shook their heads.

Ellen watched Colter as he walked away from the circle of firelight. The tall, ramrod-straight figure faded into the shadows like a specter. Who is this man? Where had he come from? He was so different from others she had seen out west. She was impressed with how he took command of the situation. Ellen sensed a toughness about him, but at the same time a caring for people. She liked that in a man. This stranger stirred dormant feelings she had thought would never return. She was secretly embarrassed and angry with herself for having these thoughts about a man she didn't know. Colter returned with his horse. The bond between man and animal was evident. She glimpsed Colter's smile when the horse nuzzled him. Her heartbeat quickened at the handsome smile.

Colter looped the reins over a low-hanging cottonwood limb and removed the saddle. With clumps of wheatgrass, he meticulously rubbed down Smoke, and then brought the saddle near the fire.

The campfire licked at the night. Shadows danced as cottonwoods hovered over them. An aura of peace had settled on each face. Colter settled back, awaiting Radison's return. Would the Sioux try a sneak attack? Yeager had his men posted, so he dismissed the thought. The moon sliver illuminated the prairie about them, its light reflecting in the pool. Stars shrouded the prairie like tiny candles. Ellen sighed, thinking it was the most beautiful sight she had ever seen. Diffidently, she looked askance at Colter. He was watching her and quickly averted his gaze. She smiled and felt the thump of her heart.

Chapter Five

Radison's hand moved to his cedar-butted Colt as he warily approached the stagecoach. Yeager had posted one of his men, but there were three figures.

One of the men challenged, "Sheriff Radison?"

"Yeah, it's Radison. See ya got them bodies ready," he said, while watching the two figures leaning against the coach.

Yeager's man gestured. "Sheriff, this here's two of Major Frank North's Pawnee soldiers, Little Raven and Johnny Hawk. They said if you need 'em, they can help you take the bodies to Cheyenne."

The Pawnees nodded. Radison said, "I'll take ya up on that. It'd be hard to handle them two bodies alone. 'Sides, I'd like the company."

Radison slipped off his mount, reached inside a pocket for the makings, and built a quirly. Cupping his hands, he lit up and drew deep while eyeing the two Pawnees. In the moonlight, Radison could make little of their features. Both wore a headband with shoulder-length braided hair. One

was rangy, the other shorter and barrel-chested with powerful arms. He knew of Major North and his Pawnee soldiers.
It was their job to watch for the Sioux, Cheyenne, Arapaho,
or others who wanted to avenge the white man's encroach-
ment. General Dodge didn't want another derailment like
the one at Plum Creek.

Radison's eyes swung around the horizon. He drew hard
on the quirly and took the reins of his horse. "Okay, Little
Raven and Johnny Hawk, let's mount up. We got to git to
Cheyenne and back by midnight."

The Pawnees had fashioned a hackamore for each horse
from rope they found on the stage. Little Raven and Johnny
Hawk sprang onto their horses. Each led a horse by a
lead rope. The Pawnees were well armed with Spencers,
sidearms, and hunting knives. Radison crawled into the
saddle, raised an arm, and motioned forward.

Little Raven and Johnny Hawk pushed ahead, moving
silently, like shadows. The Pawnees' braided hair danced on
their shoulders. Seemingly, they knew every ridge and boulder. Within two hours, they topped a rise and saw the lights
of Cheyenne.

Radison and the Pawnees pulled up in front of the Union
Pacific office, swung down, and looped the reins over a hitching rail. Radison's horse was spent, but the Pawnee mounts
were still fresh. Major North wanted horses with stamina
and that's what he got.

A single lantern cast a dim light in the Union Pacific office. Weems was sleeping in a chair that leaned back precariously while his feet rested on the table. Radison slapped
a hand on the table. Weems jerked awake and tumbled over
backwards. After scrambling to his feet, embarrassment and
then anger flushed his face.

He glared at Radison, rubbed sleep from his eyes, and

scowled, "Who are you? What do you mean comin' in here—"

"Listen, mister, I ain't in no mood for talk. I'm Sheriff Luke Radison from Lodgepole. Me and Marshal Colter found the stage 'bout two hours out, ambushed by Sioux. Soldiers from Fort Russell showed up just in time to rescue 'em." He thumbed over his shoulder. "I've got the driver and guard outside, both dead. The passengers are all right 'cept for some bruises. One's got a broke arm. I need another stage to go out and pick up them people, or another wheel to replace the one that got busted, and three horses."

Weems, sobered by the news, said, "Jessup and Ashton both dead?"

Radison impatiently retorted, "That's right."

Radison pulled his hat low over his eyes and glared at Weems. The Union Pacific man squirmed and gathered himself. "Sheriff, we ain't got a stage, but I can get you another wheel and the horses you need, and you'll need a buckboard to carry that wheel in."

Radison nodded. "Yeah. I need 'em right away. We got to git back there by midnight."

Weems asked, skeptically, "You gonna bring 'em in tonight?"

"If the passengers feel up to it."

Radison heard the commotion and a slurred voice. "You thievin' Injuns, what did ya do? Kill Ike and Pete?"

Radison darted out of the tent to see a burly, whiskered man threatening Little Raven. The man's hand moved to the Dragoon Colt jammed inside his belt.

"Hold it, mister!"

Radison moved quickly and shoved his Colt in the big man's belly. Dwarfing Radison, he reeked of whiskey, tobacco, and stale sweat. The lazy left eye wandered while the other leered at the sheriff.

Radison nudged the Colt deeper into the man's belly. "I said back off, mister. Little Raven and Johnny Hawk helped save the passengers. Jessup and Ashton was done for when they got there."

The man grunted in disgust, threw up his hands, and backed away. Curious onlookers gathered and gawked at the bodies.

Radison looked over the crowd. "Listen folks, I need somebody to take care of them bodies."

A gangly, pasty-faced man in black stepped forward, staring impassively. "I'll take care of 'em."

"Thanks, mister." Radison continued, "Does anybody know a Chester and Susan York?"

A stifled cry arose from somewhere in the growing crowd. The people parted and a couple stepped forward. The man's hair and pencil mustache were neatly trimmed. The bonnet-clad woman at his side was slight of stature with a pinched mouth that quivered in anticipation.

"That's us, Sheriff," Chester York said haltingly.

"Mr. York, Miz Usrey is all right. She's a little shook up, that's all. There's soldiers and Marshal Colter with 'em. If the passengers are willin', we'll bring 'em in tonight. If not, we'll be in tomorrow."

Susan York put a hand to her mouth and sobbed, "Oh, thank God!"

Radison swung his attention back to the crowd. "I need somebody to go to Lodgepole and tell Miz Wellsley what happened and that her daughter is all right."

A U.S. Cavalry officer rode into the circle of light, revealing a tanned and handsome face. Smartly dressed, he steadied his mount and raised his hand.

The officer's voice was strong and authoritative. "Sheriff, I'm Captain Kilbane from Fort Russell. I'll send some men right away. What's the young lady's name, and where will they find Mrs. Wellsley?"

"Ellen Wellsley, Captain. They'll find Miz Wellsley at Wellsley's Boardin' House."

Kilbane leaned forward in the saddle. "Sheriff, did you say Ellen Wellsley?"

"That's right, Captain. Somethin' wrong?"

"No, Sheriff, there's no problem."

Kilbane's interest was piqued, recalling an Ellen Wellsley he had met four years before. Turning, he said, "Corporal Quigley, you and Private Zeman get over to Lodgepole and let Mrs. Wellsley know what's going on."

Radison said, "Thank you, Captain. Now, one more thing. Is there anybody here who can drive a stage?"

"I can."

Radison turned to see the man who had threatened Little Raven and asked, "Are ya up to it, mister?"

"Name's Coop Ivey," he said, hitching up his baggy pants. "Yeah, I can handle it."

Radison looked the crowd over and didn't see another choice. "All right, Ivey. Ya better git some coffee in ya. We'll be pullin' out in a few minutes. You'll drive the buckboard. Where's Weems?"

"Right here, Sheriff. Got your board, wheel, and horses ready to go."

"Good. I'm gonna git me another mount, and then we'll be ready to go."

Radison lit a quirly, drew deep, and headed for the livery.

"Howdy, Sheriff."

Radison turned his head to see a lanky stranger leaning

against a post. The man cupped a match in his left hand, lighting a quirly. His right hand rested on the butt of the gun in a holster tied low on his right leg. The flame outlined the thin face and wide-set eyes.

Radison said, "Do I know you, mister?"

"Not yet. New to these parts. Was passin' through, but I think I'll stay a while."

The stranger turned with a lingering stare, then made his way down the boardwalk and turned up an alley.

Radison stepped off the boardwalk, noting the big dun with a fancy rig. He figured the Pawnees would each lead a horse; the other horse would follow behind the buckboard.

Near midnight, Jed Colter moved quietly about camp. Tired but restless, he figured Radison would return soon. His eyes traversed the camp and came to rest on Ellen. She was at peace as rest worked its magical powers. She was on his mind, more than he cared to admit.

When he heard voices, Colter stealthily moved out of the circle of firelight. His hand dropped to the Colt, and then a rider approached through the willows. Radison had kept his promise.

Radison eased wearily from the saddle. "Jed, we got everthin' to git the passengers goin'. Two of Major North's Pawnee soldiers helped me git Jessup and Ashton to Cheyenne. Don't know if I coulda done it alone. Ya wanna start 'em tonight?"

"Yes, I'll wake the passengers and get them ready. Did you get another stage?"

Radison shook his head. "No, we brung a wheel. Yeager and his men are fixin' it. Found a driver in Cheyenne. Fella named Ivey. He was liquored up, but I think he's sober 'nough by now. Found the Yorks and told 'em 'bout Miz

Usrey. A U.S. Cavalry Captain Kilbane sent two of his men
to tell Ma 'bout Miss Ellen."

"Kilbane? Bert Kilbane?"

Radison shrugged. "Didn't give his full name. Ya got any
coffee made?"

"Yes, its on the fire." Colter passed Radison a tin cup and
asked, "Describe this Kilbane."

"Best I could tell, he was 'bout six feet, thick in the chest,
and a slim waist. Spoke with plenty of authority. Looked to
be 'bout your age."

Radison lit a quirly with the glowing end of a stick. He
reached for the coffeepot and filled the cup. Ellen began to
toss and turn in her bedroll.

"No! No!" Ellen screamed.

Two steps and Colter was by Ellen's side, gently shaking
her. Fearful, Ellen pulled herself close to him, then quickly
let go, realizing what she had done. Colter's heart pounded.

Ellen looked away, embarrassed. "I had a bad dream,
Marshal. I'm sorry."

Colter smiled. "No need to be sorry, Miss Ellen. How
about some water or coffee?"

Ellen's eyes met Colter's. "I think I'll try your coffee."

"I can't lay claim to the coffee, but I've got some of your
mother's biscuits in my saddlebag if you want to try one."

Ellen laughed softly. Curiosity and bewilderment mingled on her face. "My mother's biscuits? Where did you get
my mother's biscuits?"

Colter wanted to crawl into a hole and gather his wits.
Ellen's smile, to his way of thinking, lit up the whole prairie.
He returned with Ma's biscuits and poured a cup of coffee.

Ellen took the coffee and biscuit, lifted her chin, and
said, "Now tell me about these biscuits, Marshal Colter."

He swallowed hard. "Well, first of all, everybody who

knows your mother calls her Ma, because she's like a mother to them. When I go out on the trail, she insists I take some food with me. It's a relief from what a man usually has when he's out here alone."

Ellen hesitantly took a bite of the biscuit. She nodded. "Yes, these are mother's biscuits. No one makes biscuits like my mother." She peered at Colter over the rim of the cup, taking her first sip of trail coffee. "And the coffee is good too."

Colter smiled, questions peppering his mind. Why wasn't she married? Or was she? Ma hadn't said one way or another. He didn't see a wedding ring. It was obvious she could have any man of her choosing. She had plenty of spirit, and she just might fit in out here.

Ellen thought of David Easton. He had cut quite a figure in his uniform. That's the way she would remember him. But this Colter. What is it about him that intrigued her? It was like he came from another life and was dropped here on this prairie. He was disciplined and handled himself like a military man. A handsome, rugged man, his smile stripped away the sadness in her life and brought a blush to her cheeks. Enigmatic thoughts slithered into her mind. She grew melancholy watching the flames push back the darkness.

The passengers moved about as Radison hunkered by the fire, mesmerized by the dancing spires and red-hot coals. Finishing his coffee, he took a draw on the quirly and flipped it into the fire. He took note of the banter going on between Colter and Ellen Wellsley. Twisting his handlebar mustache, Radison grinned, then grew pensive as memories of another life inundated his thoughts.

Colter said, "We've got a few biscuits, coffee, and water if any of you want some."

This time, there were takers. Singleton smiled and raised his cup. "Very tasty, Marshal."

Colter asked, "How's that arm, Mr. Singleton?"

"It feels surprisingly well, Marshal. Thank you very much."

Colter tossed the last of his coffee into the fire. "The stage should be ready to roll. Do any of you want to spend the night here, or do you want to go on to Cheyenne? It's a two- to three-hour ride."

Singleton said, "We're game, Marshal." The others nodded in agreement.

"Sheriff, did you bring a buckboard?" Colter asked.

"Yeah. I'll bring it to the willows."

"Sergeant Yeager, have your men gather up these bedrolls and slickers. We'll meet Sheriff Radison just beyond those willows, and he'll take you folks to the stage."

As Colter grabbed his bedroll and saddle, he heard, "Better watch that filly. She'll rope and hawgtie ya."

Colter turned to see Radison grinning. Speechless, he watched the sheriff mount and vanish into the night. He considered Radison's warning, then smiled and shook his head.

Colter saddled Smoke, then poured the remaining coffee on the dying fire and scattered the coals.

"Plummer, pour some water over these coals, and then cover them up with dirt."

"Yes, sir."

After Plummer had doused the fire, Colter tested the coals with his boot toe.

"Good work, Plummer. Folks, let's move over beyond those willows."

Radison and the buckboard were waiting as Colter and the passengers emerged from the willows. After all had crawled onto the buckboard, Colter followed alongside. His eyes scanned the moonlit prairie for any sign of trouble.

Yeager's men had replaced the wheel and put the team in harness. Colter dismounted and spotted the two Pawnees.

Colter asked, "Which one of you is Little Raven?"

"That me; that Johnny Hawk," responded the taller of the two.

"Little Raven and Johnny Hawk, I'm Jed Colter, Deputy United States Marshal from Lodgepole. I want to thank you for what you've done here. I'll make sure that Major North knows about it."

At the mention of the name Colter, Little Raven and Johnny Hawk exchanged glances.

Ellen watched curiously from a distance. She didn't hear all that was said, but she did hear Johnny Hawk say, "The name Colter carries great honor among all tribes."

What did Johnny Hawk mean by that? What had this man done that his name would be honored among the tribes? Even the Sioux? The ones who had attacked the stage and killed Jessup and Ashton? Ellen's inquisitive mind turned over these thoughts as she stepped into the stage.

Little Raven pointed and said, "Little Raven and Johnny Hawk scout ahead."

Colter waved acknowledgment and stepped into the saddle. Ellen heard the awe and respect in the Pawnee's voice.

Coop Ivey was checking the team as Colter approached.

"Ivey, you able to drive this rig?" Colter asked dubiously.

With labored breathing, Ivey said, "Ya bet, Marshal. I won't let ya down."

Ivey climbed aboard and took the reins. His speech was clear, and he mounted the stage in a way that made Colter feel better.

Colter took a look around and held up an arm. "Ivey, I think we're ready. Let's go!"

"Yii, git up, ya varmits! Let's finish the job Ike and Pete started."

The stage creaked and rocked back and then forward. Colter heard the lighthearted chatter among the passengers. They moved steadily across the plains as Little Raven and Johnny Hawk scouted ahead. Radison followed the stage in the buckboard, and Yeager rode ahead while two of his men brought up the rear on either side. Colter rode alongside, occasionally dropping back to talk with Radison.

Three hours later, they crested a rise and saw a sprinkling of lights ahead. Colter pulled alongside the stage.

"Cheyenne up ahead!" Colter yelled.

"Oh, thank God!" Singleton shouted.

Colter smiled. He liked the Englishman's grit.

Chapter Six

A sleepy-eyed Weems greeted Colter. "Marshal, got some bad news for you. That Corporal Quigley who went to tell Miz Wellsley about her daughter came back a while ago and said the bank at Lodgepole was robbed yesterday."

Colter looped the reins over the hitching rail and thought of the stranger Asa Longley had told him about. He was angry with himself for leaving Lodgepole unprotected. But what else could he have done? Radison had to take that prisoner to Cheyenne and he had to meet Miss Ellen. Maybe he should have taken the prisoner and left Radison to look out after the town. It was too late now; the deed was done.

"Mr. Weems, did he give any details?"

"He said the banker, I believe it was a Mr. Nenquist, was shot, but he's still alive. Don't know how much money was took. Didn't have any other details, no description of who done it."

"Is Corporal Quigley still around?"

"Don't think so, Marshal. I believe him and that Captain Kilbane went back to Fort Russell."

"The stage is right behind me. Those folks will need beds to rest up."

"Already took care of that, Marshal. The Grand Prairie Hotel down the street is expectin' you folks."

Colter searched for the Grand Prairie Hotel. He passed several tents and a frame building before getting to the clapboard structure. The sign out front touted the hotel as the *Best on the Plains.* Light spilled out onto the boardwalk from the lobby where the night clerk busied himself in preparation for the passengers.

Colter heard the clatter of the stagecoach and then saw the team swing wide around a corner. Lamps were lit by the curious. Colter stepped off the boardwalk and waved his arms. Ivey saw him and guided the stage to a stop.

"Good work, Ivey," Colter said, reaching for the stage door. "Folks, the Grand Prairie Hotel is expecting you. I'll see about getting a doctor."

Singleton said, "Marshal, you and Miss Ellen have done a splendid job. As for Mrs. Singleton and me, the doctor can wait." Others muttered their agreement.

Colter helped each passenger off the stage. Ellen offered her hand as she stepped to the ground. Her hand lingered in his for a moment and, with a slight squeeze, she looked up at him from tired eyes.

"Thank you, Marshal Colter, for all you've done."

Colter touched his hat brim. "Ma'am, I'm sorry for all that's happened."

"What time will we leave for Lodgepole?"

"You need rest. We can leave when you're ready. Your mother has been notified, so she knows you're all right."

Ellen cocked her head to one side, looked up at Colter, and with a weary smile entered the hotel.

Colter found Radison talking with the Pawnees while drawing on a quirly.

"Luke, the bank at Lodgepole was robbed yesterday. Mr. Nenquist was shot, but word is he's still alive."

Radison's eyes flashed anger. He took the last draw on his quirly and dropped it to the ground. "I'm leavin' now. Marshal, I suggest that Little Raven and Johnny Hawk go with you to take Miss Ellen to Lodgepole." The Pawnees nodded.

The weary Radison changed to the buckskin he had brought over from Lodgepole. He climbed into the saddle and nudged his mount toward Lodgepole. Colter wondered which would make it, the buckskin or Radison.

Yeager approached and said, "Marshal, if ya don't need us anymore, we'll head back to Fort Russell."

Colter shook his head. "Sergeant Yeager, I believe you've done all you can do. Thank you and your men for taking care of those people."

Yeager took the hand Colter offered, then tugged on a glove. "Jus' part of the job, Marshal."

"Sergeant, one other thing. Is there a Captain Bert Kilbane at Fort Russell?"

"Yep. Fine officer too."

"Tell him Jed Colter said hello."

Colter smiled and his spirits lifted. It would be good renewing the friendship with Kilbane. Maybe he would know something about Dave Easton.

After taking Smoke to the livery, Colter threw his saddlebags over a shoulder and picked up the key to room five. He wrestled fatigue and trudged up the stairs. Colter stepped through the door, struck a match, and lit the lamp on a bedside table. A larger table with a basin and pitcher of water stood by the opposite wall. A breeze gently furled the curtain as Colter parted it with a finger and looked down on the deserted street. He unbuckled his gunbelt and hung it over a bedpost. After removing his boots, he poured water into the basin and splashed his face to remove the dust and sweat. Soon sleep overtook him amid thoughts of Ellen Wellsley.

The eastern horizon lay in a blanket of orange and lilac when Radison tapped on Dr. Aiden Burke's door.

"Come in, it's open."

Radison found Doc Burke sitting at a table he used as a desk. A window overlooked the boardwalk and Main Street. Stacks of medical books and assorted papers covered his desk, nearly obscuring a woman's photograph. An arched top bracket clock and candles were centered on the mantel. The overstuffed chair in a corner provided Doc comfort in his leisure time. Burke practiced his skills in a private room to the rear, backed by sleeping quarters and a small kitchen.

Burke looked up over glasses that sat on the end of his nose. No one in town seemed to know anything about him, nor was he free with information. He had shown up along with others who settled in Lodgepole. In his early fifties, Burke was a short but solid man with a smooth, clean-shaven face. Burke removed his glasses and, with a grunt, stood up. He ran a thumb under his suspenders and hitched up his pants.

"Sheriff, if you're here to see Mr. Nenquist, you're too late. He died about two hours ago. Shot three times, and he wasn't even armed." Burke shook his head in disgust.

Radison hooked a thumb in his gunbelt. "Doc, did he say anythin'?"

"He lost consciousness right after we got him here. All he said was, 'droopy eyes.' "

Perplexed, Radison pushed back his hat and asked, "Droopy eyes?"

"All I can figure is the fella that shot him must've had droopy eyes."

"Anybody else see anythin'?"

"Don't know, Sheriff. Maybe Mrs. Nenquist or Mr. Vick over at the dry goods store or Asa Longley."

He didn't like the idea of talking to Mrs. Nenquist, but it would have to be done. Vick hadn't seen much, but he did hear shots and saw a stranger hurriedly ride out of town.

In haste, Radison had left his jaded horse in front of Burke's office. The reins dangled free, but the buckskin wasn't going anywhere. Running a hand over the buckskin's neck, Radison said softly, "C'mon, boy, I feel porely for puttin' you through that."

Radison took a slow walk to Longley's Livery. "Asa, give him water and grain him. He's had a rough night. And rub him down too," he said, then asked, "Asa, did ya see the fella that kilt Mr. Nenquist?"

"Might have, Sheriff." Longley spit and wiped a hand across his mouth. "That fella with the fancy rig come high-tailin' it down the street a laughin' right after I hear'd them shots. Headed toward Cheyenne."

"Did this fella have droopy eyes?"

Reaching for a bucket, Longley suddenly turned. "Yeah, he did! That's him! A lanky, ugly fella. Look's like a snake."

Radison thought of the gunslick he had seen in Cheyenne and the horse with the fancy rig. He was Nenquist's killer! Radison remembered the stranger's insolent look. The man had said he was passing through but then decided to stay.

What changed his mind? Radison wondered if he had anything to do with the man's decision to stay. If so, why?

Radison was spent. He headed for Ma's, and then he would rest before Colter and Miss Ellen arrived.

Colter awoke with a start. Light filtered through the window curtain. He was an early riser, but exhaustion had won the battle. He got up, looked into the dusty mirror over the water basin and saw two days of black stubble. He mumbled, "Miss Ellen must have thought I was a saddle tramp." Finding a razor and soap in a saddlebag, he raked off the whiskers in long easy strokes.

After buckling his gunbelt, Colter grabbed his hat and saddlebags. Descending the stairs, he caught the scent of steak. Colter took a seat by a window overlooking the boardwalk. Somewhere a clock struck ten. Buckboards and supply wagons made a steady stream of traffic along the street.

A shrill voice asked, "What can I git'cha, Mister?"

Colter looked up to see a stout, round-faced woman who wore an apron with the embroidered words *Grand Prairie Hotel Welcomes You* across the front.

"Steak and eggs and a pot of coffee."

Colter finished the steak and eggs and then drained the last cup of coffee. He was leaning back in the chair when he saw Ellen standing at the foot of the stairs. Her hair was tightly pulled back into a bun at the rear. A black, wide-brimmed hat sloped down on her forehead. Dark pants and a white blouse with a black string-ribbon tied in a bow at the neck accentuated her slender figure and graceful curves. Ellen Wellsley was the most beautiful woman he had ever seen.

Colter smiled, removing his hat. "Good morning, Miss Ellen."

She returned his smile. "Good morning to you, Marshal."

Embarrassed, he said, "I apologize for my appearance."

"You look fine, Marshal. I understand the circumstances."

Mesmerized by Colter's blue eyes that seemed to penetrate her soul, Ellen admired his square jaw and wide smile. She wanted to know more about this stranger and would before the day was done.

Colter asked, "Have you had anything to eat?"

"No, I haven't."

"While you eat, I'll get a buckboard ready."

The liveryman hitched a gentle mare to a buckboard. Colter saddled Smoke and tied the reins to the rear of the buckboard. He climbed aboard, flicked the reins, and drove to the Grand Prairie. Colter entered the lobby and sought out the desk clerk.

He asked, "Has Miss Wellsley's luggage been brought down?"

"Yes, sir, it's over there," he said, pointing to several bags and boxes.

"Are you ready, Marshal?"

Colter turned to see Ellen. "We'll leave at your convenience, ma'am."

She said anxiously, "I'm ready."

Grabbing bags and boxes, Colter and the clerk loaded Ellen's luggage onto the buckboard. Little Raven and Johnny Hawk lounged near their ponies.

Colter caught the fragrance of Ellen's perfume when he helped her up to the seat. Her blushed, full lips smiled. Colter's heart raced, and he thought about what Radison had said. But why would a lady like Miss Ellen be interested in him?

Colter grabbed the Henry and climbed aboard. With a flick of the reins, they were off to Lodgepole. Colter checked the sun's position and figured they would get to Lodgepole by mid-afternoon. Little Raven and Johnny Hawk mounted and took their positions out front. Their eyes constantly strayed to Colter. The jovial Johnny Hawk's wide cheekbones and beaklike nose gave him a hawklike appearance, while the poker-faced Little Raven rode in silence.

The buckboard's clatter broke the silence as Ellen's eyes surveyed the land. Captivated by its awesome expanse, she beheld an unusual beauty unlike anything she had ever seen. Thoughts of the stranger beside her were unsettling. Ellen made her decision. She would have to make the first move.

Ellen fixed her eyes ahead. "I will not call you Marshal Colter if you will call me Ellen."

Colter aroused from his thoughts. "Jed. Call me Jed."

She cocked her head to one side. "Would that be Jedidiah?"

Surprised, he said, "Yes. My father named me from the Bible." He liked the way *Jedidiah* rolled off her tongue.

"It means Beloved of The Lord. It's the same name that God commanded the prophet Nathan to call Solomon because the Lord loved him."

Colter was speechless. His father had read the Bible regularly, so he was not surprised to have a name from the Bible. She must be a reader of the Written Word.

Ellen turned to Colter and added, "Jedidiah. It's a strong name. Your father named you well."

Colter squirmed and flicked the reins. One of the Pawnees topped a rise. His pony, in full stride, left a trail of dust in its wake that caught the ubiquitous plains wind and dissipated. Colter's heart pounded. There was trouble ahead.

The Pawnee and his horse worked together as one. Ellen

grew tense as Johnny Hawk pulled up next to the buck-board. Hawk pointed north where Colter saw five riders on the crest of a ridge.

"Keep movin'! Don't stop!" Hawk said as Little Raven came into view and soon pulled up alongside.

Colter followed Hawk's advice. He reached for the Henry and placed it across his legs. The Pawnees rested the Spencers, butt end, on a thigh.

Casually, the riders approached. Soon Colter's fears were realized. Indians! If they wanted scalps, they didn't show it. Did they want horses, or even worse, did they want Ellen? Was this a trick? Were there others coming from another direction? Colter checked the terrain and then scanned the horizon, but he didn't see any others. Ellen gripped his arm.

"Whatever you do, don't show them any fear," Colter said softly. She loosened her grip on his arm, raised her chin, and defiantly held her gaze on the approaching riders.

Little Raven and Johnny Hawk moved out to meet the Indians. Colter kept the pace and his eyes on the braves. An Indian raised his right hand. Little Raven talked, and then suddenly they looked toward the buckboard. Sweat trickled down Colter's face. After Little Raven pointed, the Indians turned their mounts to the south. Raven and Hawk watched until the Indians disappeared over a ridge.

After returning to the buckboard, Raven said, "Arapaho huntin' party. Told 'em 'bout game we saw back on Lodge-pole Creek."

Hawk grinned. "Told 'em you Colter."

Ellen had seen the reaction of the Indians. Was it the men-tion of Colter's name? It pricked her curiosity.

Little Raven led the way while Johnny Hawk dropped off to check the back trail. The cunning Arapaho wouldn't miss an opportunity to make the white man pay for encroaching on their land.

Ellen glanced at Colter. She had to know. Raising her chin, she asked, "Why is the name Colter so respected among the Indians?"

Colter laughed. Ellen turned and faced him, wondering if she should have asked the question.

"It may seem a bit farfetched, but you did ask."

A smile played on her lips. At last she would learn something of this man who crowded her thoughts.

Colter said, "You've heard of Lewis and Clark and their expeditions out west?"

"Yes."

Colter continued. "There was a John Colter who traveled with Lewis and Clark and helped them make maps of the Northwest. I'm told he was my Grandfather Colter's brother, and I do remember some tall tales about him. One in particular they say is true."

Colter paused and Ellen squirmed impatiently. "It seems that Uncle John and a trapper friend intruded on Blackfoot territory while trapping and were captured."

"Who are the Blackfoot?"

"Blackfoot Indians, a fierce fighting people. Some say they got their name because the soles of their moccasins were black from walking across burned prairie."

Ellen nodded.

"The trapper resisted the Blackfoot, even killed one of their leaders, so the Blackfoot killed him while Uncle John looked on. They stripped Uncle John down to where he didn't have any clothes on, and then challenged him to a foot race through the wilderness. If he won, he got to live; if he lost, he died. They gave him a short head start, and then all the young bucks took out after him, through thickets, rivers, mountains, and prairies. It's been reported they ran well over a hundred miles before the last buck gave up. Word got around to other tribes, and pretty soon it was used as a symbol of courage among the Indians. The Indian respects those who show courage in battle, be they white or red."

Ellen realized her mouth had gaped open. "That's the most amazing feat I've ever heard. What happened to your Uncle John?"

"He finally settled and started a family somewhere in Missouri. I heard he died in St. Louis."

Colter figured he had talked enough. He asked, "Now, what brings you out here?"

"It's a long story, but I'll try to make it short."

He detected despair in her voice. It troubled him because of the spirit she had shown. He looked askance and saw Ellen's hands balled into fists on her lap.

Colter said, "You don't have to talk about it."

Suddenly, she looked at him. "Oh, no! I–I want to. I need to."

She continued. "Mother and Father sent me to a young ladies' boarding school in Baltimore. It was there I met a young man from West Point. He was very handsome and dashing with a brilliant future. We fell in love."

Abruptly, Ellen grabbed Colter's arm and pointed. "Oh look! How beautiful!"

Before them was a panorama of cliffs, layered in varying shades of reds and browns and burnished by the plains sun. Ellen relaxed as she took in the view.

"It must be magnificent at sunset. One day will you bring me out for a sunset?"

Colter smiled. "Sure."

"Anyway," Ellen continued, "we were to be married. On the day before our wedding, David was called to report for battle at Gettysburg. We had to put off our wedding until he could get enough time off. I received one letter from him, and then word came that he had died in battle. I'll never forget the lieutenant who brought the news. He was so young and near tears when he told me of David's death. I believe he was a classmate of David's at West Point." She paused and reflected. "His name was Kilbane."

In defiance of the unrelenting heat of the high plains sun, a chill swept over Colter like an eerie fog. It was the moment he feared would someday come.

"David?"

Colter barely got the name out, reminding him of the day he resigned from West Point.

"Easton," Ellen replied.

Chapter Seven

Colter grimly surveyed the horizon ahead. Ellen sensed something was wrong.

"What's wrong?"

"Dave was my closest friend at West Point. We were like brothers."

Ellen gasped. "So *you're* Jed!"

Colter smiled. "And you're the young lady Dave said he was going to marry! He told me in his last letter, but he never mentioned your name."

Ellen gathered herself. "I don't know what to say. David told me so much about you."

She thought about the coincidence of meeting David's best friend under these remarkable circumstances. She believed in fate. Suddenly, Ellen's heart pounded and her eyes glistened. She pondered the feelings this man had awakened in her. Now she understood why. The qualities she saw in Colter were the same that had attracted her to Easton.

Colter was saddened by the news of Dave's death, but a

part of his friend was sitting by him. Suddenly, he felt a bond to Ellen. He smiled, remembering Dave had brought the prettiest girl to every dance.

"Why are you smiling?"

"Dave would—"

"Dave would what?"

Sheepishly he said, "He had a knack for picking the prettiest girl."

Colter swallowed, feeling the flush in his face.

"Oh? There were other girls?" Ellen playfully asked.

Colter stammered, "That was before you came along."

Ellen cocked her head, smiling wryly as she looked sidewise at Colter. "What about Jed Colter? Did he show up at the dance with a pretty girl?"

"Sometimes."

Ellen visualized Colter in his cadet uniform. She pursed her lips and said, "Somehow I think Cadet Colter had his pick of the ladies."

Colter squirmed, thinking of a way to change the subject. "Say, how did Dave finish at the Point?"

"Second in his class. He said you would have finished first had you stayed."

"I'm not so sure of that. We were neck and neck."

"He told me why you left West Point. It must have been a hard decision."

Colter nodded, seemingly not wanting to talk about it.

The red sandstone boulders came into view. Colter said, "Lodgepole just ahead."

Colter eased the buckboard alongside the boardwalk by Wellsley's Boarding House. He wrapped the reins around the brake and stepped down.

"Ellen! Ellen! Thank God you're here!" Ma shouted.

After Ma and Ellen embraced, Ma reached out and tugged at Colter's sleeve. "Thank you, Jed."

It pleased Ma the way Ellen looked at Colter.

Colter shook off the prairie dust, grabbed bags and boxes, and took them up to Ellen's room. After he had finished with the luggage, he took the buckboard to the livery.

Before unhitching the mare, Asa Longley said, "Marshal, that lanky, ugly cuss with the fancy rig robbed and kilt Mr. Nenquist."

"Mr. Nenquist is dead?"

"That's right, Marshal."

Longley recounted what he had told Radison.

"Thanks, Asa," Colter said, leaving for Ma's.

When Colter stuck his head in the door, Ma said, "Jed, your bath water is waiting."

"Thanks, Ma."

He ascended the stairs and went to his room. A breeze rustled the window curtain. The ambient air smelled of fresh sheets. Sir William Blackstone's *Commentaries* were placed neatly on a table in the soft glow of a kerosene lamp. Many frontier lawyers had used *Commentaries* to educate themselves in the law. Ma had brought in an armoire her husband had used. A basin and pitcher of water sat on a chest of drawers with an upright mirror.

Colter shucked his dusty, sweat-drenched clothes and stepped into a tub of tepid water. After bathing, he shaved and dressed before joining Ellen and Ma at a table by a window.

Six evenly spaced tables with blue-and-white checkerboard tablecloths filled the small dining area that accommodated boarders. Occasionally, other merchants would drop in for a meal. A crusty old trail cook did most of the cooking, except for the pies. That was Ma's specialty. A loud, vociferous protest was heard whenever Ma checked the food for proper seasoning.

Ma said, "Have a seat, young man, and I'll get you some food."

Colter took a chair opposite Ellen as Ma brought a cup of coffee. He noted a twinkle in Ma's eyes he had not seen before. Her mischievous smile made him uneasy. Like a Pawnee tracker, Ma could read signs, and she was pleased.

"Jed, I must tell you of something I saw in Omaha. At the end of track, I saw these same men and one other. I'm not sure if it means anything." Ellen told Colter of the wagon being loaded on the train at Omaha, the prisoners, the lawman, and Harley Banes.

Colter leaned forward, attentive. "Did you get a look at this lawman?"

"Mr. Banes called him Sheriff Farnsworth. He's a big man, about six feet, and at least two hundred pounds, red hair, red face, and his left earlobe is missing."

Colter recalled what Ebetts had told him and struck the table with a fist.

"Gibbons! That has to be Gibbons!"

Startled, Ellen asked, "Who is Gibbons?"

"Sergeant Abe Gibbons. He was in charge of guard detail at a Union Army prison camp. Gibbons apparently deserted the same time some of the prisoners disappeared along with my father."

Colter told Ellen of his search for his father. Intensity and a sense of purpose blanketed his face.

Ma hustled from the kitchen with a plate of steak and potatoes.

"Don't let me stop you two from talking."

Ma giggled, wheeled about, and headed for the kitchen.

"Do you think one of those prisoners could be your father?"

"I'd bet on it. How many prisoners did you see?"

"Four."

Ebetts told him there were four other men who had disappeared along with his father. Where was the fifth?

"Tell me about Banes and the other man you saw him with at the end of track. Describe them."

"This Harley Banes said he was a construction boss for the Union Pacific. I would say near six feet, two hundred pounds. His face was lined and very tan, streaky gray hair, crooked front teeth. The other man was short, powerfully built with huge arms and legs and a large torso. Wore a floppy hat and carried a whip coiled over his right shoulder."

"What did Banes say on the train?"

"He was cordial, but he got nervous when I asked about the wagon I saw those men loading onto the train in Omaha. He said they were prisoners being sent out to the end of track to work off their time."

Finding Banes would be easy since he worked for the Union Pacific. Gibbons would be easy to spot. The other man Ellen had seen could be any of the many muleskinners around Cheyenne.

Colter was finishing his steak when Luke Radison came in, pulled up a chair, and straddled it.

"Guess ya heard?"

"Heard what?" Colter asked.

"That Mr. Nenquist died."

"Yes. We know who the killer is; we just don't have a name."

"Saw him last night in Cheyenne and that fancy rig. Even spoke to me and looked at me like he know'd me from somewhere. He'd already robbed the bank and kilt Mr. Nenquist. Doc Burke said that jasper shot Mr. Nenquist three times and Mr. Nenquist didn't even have a gun. Asa said he was laughin' when he rode out. He's a mean gunslick."

Colter turned his cup slowly, thinking about a young gunfighter he had run out of Sedalia.

"Did you get a good look at him?"

"No, it was dark. Asa's description's as good as any."

Colter took the last swallow of coffee and pushed back his chair.

"I'm leaving for Cheyenne in the morning. Luke, you stay here and see what you can turn up. Go to the Westerner's Saloon. He was there, so they might have a name. I'll be looking for him."

Radison drew on a quirly and flicked the ash.

"Be careful, Jed. I don't like the looks of that gunslick."

Colter was astir at first light. After splashing cold water on his face, he shaved, checked his gun, and grabbed his hat. The morning air was crisp. Soon the golden aspen would trumpet the coming of winter. The creak of the fifth step alerted Ma and Ellen to his coming. He settled at a table by a window.

"Good morning."

Colter looked up to see the alluring slate blue eyes and intriguing smile as Ellen poured his coffee. He caught the scent of her apple blossom perfume.

"Good morning."

Ma watched from the doorway of the kitchen as Colter and Ellen exchanged words. The look in Ellen's eyes and the way she talked about Jed brought a smile. Coming out here was good for Ellen. Jed didn't talk much about himself, so she hadn't known that he had been to West Point. Ma had liked David Easton and saw the similarities between the two.

Colter asked, "Is Ma sleeping late today?"

Ma brought the steak and eggs and huffed. "Jed Colter, I was up before your last dream."

Colter finished as Ma brought him a dozen biscuits in a cloth sack. "Thanks, Ma. Tell Radison I'm not sure when I'll be back."

Concern shrouded Ellen's face as she said softly, "Be careful."

"I will," Colter said, then left for the livery.

At Colter's approach, Longley said, " 'Bout got him ready, Jed."

"Thanks, Asa. I'll finish up."

Colter checked the cinches and reached into a pocket. Smoke tossed his head, whinnied softly, and nibbled the sugar lump from Colter's hand.

Longley shook his head. "I never see'd a cayuse take sugar like that." He grabbed a pitchfork, then added, "Ya goin' after that varmint that kilt Mr. Nenquist?"

Colter nodded. "Radison saw him in Cheyenne."

"Be careful. He's a snake if I ever saw one."

Colter, chilled by the morning air, climbed into the saddle and kneed Smoke to a brisk gallop. The sun-gilded sandstone boulders were a stark contrast against the azure-blue Wyoming sky, and shielded the lanky stranger watching him.

Radison leaned against the front wall of the jail. Slipping a hand inside his shirt, he fingered the ring hanging like a pendant from a rawhide thong, thinking of the days he had shared with Rebecca. Inexplicably, he removed the ring and put it on his finger.

After watching Colter leave the livery, Radison headed for Ma's with a peculiar feeling. Something was afoot. His eyes darted about town. Nothing seemed unusual. There were two mounts in front of Vick's and one down by the Westerner's. A buckboard rattled its way in from the north.

"Good morning, Luke."

"Mornin', Miss Ellen. Reckon ya could git Ma to rustle up some o' them biscuits?"

"I'll see what I can do."

Radison's distant, lonely eyes disturbed her. What secret did he harbor?

"Jed said to tell you he didn't know when he would be back. I hope he finds out something about his father."

Radison glanced up at Ellen. "So do I. He's been at it long enough. Jed's a good man. He'll do to ride the river with."

Ellen reflected on what Radison had said. She would ask her mother what it meant.

Radison finished off the biscuits and coffee and lit a quirly. A glance at the clock on the counter told him it was time to make the rounds. Stepping outside, he felt the chill and stretched. His eyes swept the length of Main. The odd feeling still haunted him. One of John Leach's cowhands was loading supplies on a buckboard down by Vick's. A dun had joined the other horse at the Westerner's Saloon. Remembering Longley's leg usually bothered him until the day had warmed, Radison angled toward the livery to check on the old bronc buster.

"Howdy, Sheriff."

Radison glanced at the dun and stopped. The voice was frosty. He had heard it before and was sure he had seen the dun too. Radison turned slowly, remembering he had not checked his gun. The lanky stranger stepped deliberately out of the alley by the livery, then stopped, planted his feet, and shifted his weight from one to the other. His right hand poised above the gun hanging low on his right hip. The wide-set droopy eyes and cocked smile unnerved most men. Radison was stumped. There was no doubt what this gunslick was here for. But why him? Longley was right. The man did look like a snake.

Radison glared at the stranger. He was confident he could hold his own with most, but this man had the look of a killer—the kind who enjoyed killing.

The stony-eyed Radison challenged, "Mister, I don't know who ya are, but I'm gonna take ya to jail for killin' Mr. Nenquist and robbin' the bank."

"*You're* gonna take *me* in?" the stranger scoffed, then threw back his head and laughed.

Radison was silent, watching intently, wondering, who is this man?

"Sheriff, are ya *that* good? C'mon, try it," the stranger goaded. He smiled and added, "Ya look like ya might be good with that hawgleg. Ya handled that big drunk over in Cheyenne. Maybe ya'd like to try a real gun, huh?"

"What's ya name, mister?"

"Sheriff, I'll tell ya, but ya won't live to tell about it. It's Shad Draik. Ya hung two of my brothers down in Texas for no good reason. I been trackin' ya, and now you're gonna join 'em in hell."

The thought of that day when two drunken men murdered his Rebecca angered Radison. Draik's right shoulder flinched, and then his hand brought up the gun. Radison grabbed his .44, but he felt a tug and knew something was wrong.

Draik's gun roared, ripping asunder the quiet peace of the morning. The gunshot ricocheted among the buildings and up the slopes of the valley. Radison felt the hot lead burn deep in his chest. Draik's bullet knocked him back a step. He fired from reflex, but missed. Again, Draik's gun bucked in his hand, spinning Radison around as the bullet tore into his left shoulder. His knees buckled, and the .44 slipped from his hand. Draik laughed as his Colt spat death a third time. Radison sprawled in the dusty street, a crimson stain spreading ominously across his chest and shoulder.

Draik sauntered over to where Radison lay, emptied the spent cartridges, reloaded, and holstered his gun. Looking down at Radison's still body, he smiled contemptuously.

"Sheriff," he sneered, "ya wuz a bit slow."

Chapter Eight

Harley Banes leaned back in his chair, gazing out a window. Papers littered a makeshift desk. A curtain separated his sleeping quarters, which consisted of a cot, table, and lamp. Banes shifted his gaze to the bear of a man sitting across from him. Pug Hackett, a surly man, was not fit for friend or enemy. Short and compact, he had thick arms and legs with a robust torso. Hackett leaned forward, wheezing with each breath. His body odor permeated the small office. Grinning around the stub of a cigar, Hackett burst into a gurgling laugh.

"What'sa matter, Harley? The smell too much for ya?"

"Don't ya ever take a bath?"

Hackett bared his tobacco-stained teeth and said, "I'm used to it."

In his business, he had little time for baths. He had captured runaways for slave owners. Now he had prisoners and a good deal going with Banes. Unknowingly, the Union Pacific paid the prisoners' wages. Banes kept most and gave the rest to Hackett. It kept him and his partner, Gibbons, in

69

cheap whiskey and women. It was easy living since Gibbons did most of the work.

Banes frowned. "We gotta be careful. There was a woman on the last train out who asked a lot of questions 'bout them pris'ners."

"What kinda questions?"

Banes clasped his hands behind his head and studied Hackett.

"She saw Farnsworth loadin' that wagon of yours and the pris'ners on the train at Omaha. She asked me what they'd done, where wuz they goin'. She was real curious 'bout 'em when they was unloaded here."

"Who is she?"

"Ellen Wellsley. She's a real looker." Banes paused before continuing. "Said she was meetin' somebody in Cheyenne who was takin' her to Lodgepole."

Hackett grinned and leaned back. "Now, Harley, ya ain't sweet on her, are ya?"

He resented Hackett asking about her and snapped, "Shut your mouth!"

Banes continued, "Remember, a lawman's been snoopin' 'round askin' questions 'bout somebody called Colter. I never seen him, so I don't know who he is. I told Duggan to send him on a wild goose chase out to Mesa Canyon if he comes 'round askin' 'bout this Colter fella. Maybe the Injuns will git him."

Hackett glared at Banes in disgust and sneered, "He can be bought off jes' like the rest of 'em. Don't git so nervous."

Banes glowered. "Is one of your pris'ners named Colter?"

"Yeah. I had to give him a whuppin' to git him back in line. Since then, he don't seem to know his name or the other pris'ners. Don't work like he used to. Maybe another whuppin' will git him goin' agin."

Banes stood. "I want to see them pris'ners, 'specially that Colter."

After the crew and prisoners had eaten, Gibbons had taken them away from the construction site to bed down for the night. Dusk had set in when Banes and Hackett approached the camp.

Banes pointed. "Is that Colter?"

"Yeah, that's him," Hackett snarled.

Jim Colter was shackled to a wagon wheel. A floppy hat covered a shock of salt-and-pepper hair that flowed into a gray-streaked, unkempt, chest-length beard.

Banes squatted before the prisoner. "Colter?"

Jim Colter stared vacantly at Banes from deep-set, haunting eyes.

"Are you Colter?" Banes repeated.

"He ain't been the same since that last beatin' he took," another prisoner scoffed.

"Shut up, Cain!" Hackett growled and backhanded the prisoner. Cain fell onto a prickly pear and screamed as thorns pierced his flesh.

"Hackett! Don't do that again!" Banes warned.

Banes thought about his relationship with Hackett. How did he get mixed up with this miserable wretch? He regretted the day he met Hackett in that West Virginia saloon.

Banes asked Cain, "Is his name Colter?"

Cain grimaced in pain, looked disdainfully at Hackett, then back to Banes. "Yeah. Captain James Colter."

Banes shook his head. "Hackett, ya done beat him to where he don't know his name."

"Way I see it, he had it comin'," Hackett grumbled.

Returning to the office, Banes said, "Ya need to take Colter out away from the tracks and dump him. He's no use to us in his condition."

"I don't like it," Hackett argued. "That's gonna cut into what we're makin'. Ya wanna do that?"

"We ain't got a choice. Here's what ya do. We're gittin' close to Cheyenne, and there's a lotta law there. I know of a place where there's a deposit of coal. The railroad needs that coal. I'll draw a map, so it won't be hard to find. That'll git ya 'round Cheyenne and the law, and then we can bring your men back to the tracks."

"Got any ideas where I oughta dump Colter?"

Banes hesitated. "Take him up north a ways," he replied.

Doc Burke stared intently into space and removed the stethoscope.

"He's barely alive."

"Is there a chance, Doc?" Ellen whispered.

Burke's brow furrowed. "I've never seen anybody survive wounds like these. If he makes it, it will be by the grace of God and his will to live."

Pleadingly, Ellen asked, "What can I do?"

Burke grimaced. "That bullet has got to come out of his chest. We don't have a choice. Clean up his wounds while I get ready."

Ellen moved hastily to the kitchen and soon had boiling water. While Burke sorted through medical instruments, she poured hot water into a basin, tempering it with cold water. A timorous Asa Longley appeared in the doorway, twisting his hat in trembling hands.

"Miss Ellen, is there anythin' I can do?"

Ellen carefully placed the basin of water next to Radison. "No, Mr. Longley. All we can do is clean up the wounds, get the bullet out, and hope for the best."

Longley wistfully said, "I wish Marshal Colter wuz here."

"So do I, Mr. Longley."

"I'm leavin'. If I can do anythin', please let me know."

"Thank you, I will. A prayer would help."

Backing out the door, Longley said ruefully, "Yes, ma'am."

Burke had cut away Radison's shirt, revealing a bloody torso. Seeing Radison in this condition brought back memories of the pain-racked faces of men in Union and Confederate hospitals. Ellen meticulously swabbed and cleaned Radison's wounds. A bullet had penetrated high on the right side of his chest. Fighting nausea, she checked Radison's right side. Deflected by a rib, a bullet had traveled around the side and exited the back. It was the least of his wounds, along with the shattered collarbone. Lifting Radison's arm, she hesitated. Puzzlement blanketed her face as she stared at the gold wedding band on Radison's left hand. Why hadn't she noticed it before? Where was his wife?

Burke ambled over to check Radison's wounds. "Nice work."

He rolled up his sleeves, shoved the glasses up on his nose, and cast a quizzical look at Ellen. "Is there something wrong?"

"He's wearing a wedding band. I didn't know Luke was married."

Burke frowned. "Huh? Neither did I. I've never seen a wife. He's never talked about one."

Burke lingered in thought, then said, "He's lost a lot of blood, so don't get your hopes up."

With the stethoscope, Burke searched for a heartbeat. Ellen watched the doctor's every movement and expression.

"Doc, is he—?"

Burke nodded. "He's still with us. I've got to go after that bullet, and I don't like his chances."

Burke reached for a long, pincerlike probe. Ellen turned away and closed her eyes. Clasping hands to her breast, she lifted her face toward the ceiling.

Abruptly, Ellen turned at the clinking sound as Burke dropped a bullet into the pan. Burke wiped beads of sweat from his brow, and then listened expectantly as he moved the stethoscope over Radison's chest. Finishing his examination, he drew a deep breath and expelled it slowly.

While washing his hands, Burke said, "I don't know why he's still alive. Most men would be dead."

"Is he going to make it?"

Burke grew reflective while drying his hands. "The shoulder and side wounds don't bother me. It's the chest wound. I can't tell if he's bleeding internally. He can't lose any more blood and live. If he makes it another twenty-four hours, I'll give him a fighting chance." He turned and reached for the bandages. "We need to bind up those wounds. There's nothing more we can do but wait. It's out of our hands."

After bandaging Radison, Ellen placed a hand on Burke's arm. "Doc, I'll be back to give you a rest. I'll get Mother to bring some food."

Burke glanced up from tired eyes. "Thanks. That would be nice."

She looked glumly at Radison and thought about the wedding band. What was this man's story? What about Mrs. Radison? Under those rugged features, she thought, he was a handsome man. Ellen guessed he was not much older than Jed. She placed a hand on Radison's forehead. No fever. Her hopes were heightened.

Ellen's eyes glistened. "Luke, I wish you could hear me. We really need you here."

Burke smiled. "You know, you're quite a lady. With your help, he just might make it."

"You really know how to flatter a lady." She couldn't explain it, but she felt better about Radison's chances.

A feeling of someone watching him gnawed at Jed Colter until he reached Cheyenne. Was someone getting nervous? Was he getting close to something? From Longley's description of Nenquist's killer, he had a notion who the stranger might be. Mulling over these thoughts, he pulled up at a graying clapboard building where U.S. MARSHAL'S OFFICE adorned a slightly skewed sign.

Colter stepped through the door into an outer office where the deputies attended to business. The U.S. Marshal occupied a larger office to the rear. A window overlooked the boardwalk, and the walls were bare except for Wanted posters and a line of wooden pegs for hats and coats.

"Morning, Red," Colter greeted Deputy U.S. Marshal Red Ilsen, who was seated at a desk shuffling papers. Looking younger than his thirty years, Ilsen had a band of freckles across the bridge of his nose.

"Jed, what brings you to Cheyenne?" Ilsen asked, pushing back the high-crowned hat on his carrot-colored hair.

"Looking for the critter who robbed the bank at Lodgepole and killed the banker."

Ilsen wrinkled his brow. "Oh, yeah. I heard about that. Any ideas?"

"Got a hunch, but that's all I have."

Ilsen leaned back in his chair, tapping a pencil on the desk. "Can I help?"

Colter looked over the posters on the wall, and then pulled up a chair. "You got any more Wanted posters?"

Ilsen reached in the top drawer, pulled out a stack of papers, and shoved them across the desk.

Colter thumbed through the posters, pausing to study each one. He stopped and leaned back in the chair. While scrutinizing a poster, he laid the others on the desk, and then shoved it over to Ilsen.

"That's the man. Name's Shad Draik. I ran him out of Sedalia some years back. He was a young two-bit gunslick looking to build a reputation. Killed a man in a questionable gunfight. When he refused to leave Sedalia, I kicked him in the butt, put him on his horse, and the townspeople laughed him out of town. He won't forget that."

"He'll be older and wiser," Ilsen warned.

"Draik was here in Cheyenne. Sheriff Radison saw him the night we brought in the stage. I'm going to look around. Be on the lookout for him."

Ilsen shoved the poster back to Colter. "This poster says he's wanted in Abilene for murder and bank robbery. Now he's added another notch to his gun. What's wrong with his eyes?"

"He's got droopy, wide-set eyes. Reminds me of a snake. He's got a fancy rig, and rides a big dun with a half-moon plug out of its left ear."

Colter folded the poster and put it in a shirt pocket.

"You gonna look for Draik now?"

Colter nodded. "Thought I would make the rounds. Check the saloons."

"Mind if I join you?" Ilsen asked.

Colter smiled. "I'd like that, since you know this town."

Nobody admitted knowing Draik, but Colter knew he touched a nerve at the Last Chance Saloon. The sign over the false front enticed drifters, cowhands, and railroad workers to come in and enjoy the best whiskey and the prettiest girls. The Last Chance was a typical saloon along the path of the railroad, hurriedly constructed to meet the demand. Colter and Ilsen stepped through the batwing door and paused. To the left were tables where saloon girls entertained thirsty customers and relieved them of their wages. To the right, a bar ran the length of the room. A large mirror backed the bar and over it was a painting of a reclining woman. The smell of sour whiskey, tobacco, and sweaty bodies hung in the hazy room.

Colter held up the Wanted poster. "Any of you seen this man? His name's Shad Draik. He's wanted for murder and robbing a bank in Abilene. He's also wanted for robbing the bank at Lodgepole and killing the banker."

Colter slowly walked the length of the bar. No one acknowledged his presence. He stopped where the bartender busied himself polishing a glass. "Bartender, you ever see this man?"

The bartender snapped, "Naw, I ain't seen him."

Angry, Colter reached across the bar, grabbed a handful of shirt, and dragged the startled man onto the bar.

Colter glared, his jaw clinched. "Take a good look, bartender. Have you seen this man?"

The bug-eyed bartender blurted, "I ain't seen him, Marshal!"

"You're lying!"

Colter shoved the bartender, sending him sprawling behind the bar amid broken glasses. After scrambling to his feet, he scurried to a back room. Colter spun at the click of a gun hammer and brought up his .44. Ilsen had leveled his gun at no one in particular. Suddenly, a hush descended. Colter had gotten the attention of the drifters and Union

Pacific men who had been engrossed in their favorite game of chance.

Holstering his gun, Colter moved slowly among the tables, holding up the poster. "Now, let's try this again. Has anybody seen Draik?"

Reluctantly, some looked up and shook their heads. Colter stopped at a table where a drifter and a Union Pacific man continued to play poker, seemingly oblivious to his presence.

Colter put a boot on the edge of the table and shoved. Poker chips, whiskey, and glasses scattered across the sawdust floor. The addled drifter landed on his back. Colter pounced, grabbed the man's vest, and pulled him up. His ruddy, whiskered face was frozen, and the close-set eyes grew large.

"Mister, when I ask a question, I expect an answer!"

The bewildered drifter stammered, "No, Marshal, I ain't seen this Draik."

"I know some of you, maybe all of you, are lying." Colter's gaze swung around the saloon. "Draik has been here. I can feel it. If any of you are in cahoots with him, there won't be a place on earth you can hide. You can tell Draik that Colter is coming after him."

Colter took another look around and headed for the door. A wary Ilsen backed out, then let out a sigh and holstered his gun.

"Jed," he said, smiling, "I'd say you put Draik on notice in there. He's been there all right."

"Thanks, Red. I'm glad you were with me. We missed Draik this time," Colter said, thinking of his next move. "Keep an eye on the Last Chance for me, will you? I've got some business with the Union Pacific."

Chapter Nine

Mr. Weems, do you know Harley Banes?"

Weems looked up from a stack of papers. "Yes, Marshal, he's in town. Check the Grand Prairie Hotel."

Colter quickly covered the distance to the hotel. When he arrived, he told the clerk, "I'm looking for Harley Banes."

"Yes, sir." The clerk gave Colter his best bucktooth smile and pointed to the dining area. "That's Mr. Banes over by that window."

Colter approached Banes' table and said, "Mr. Banes, I'm Jed Colter, Deputy United States Marshal."

Banes dropped his knife and looked up. His face blanched and apprehension clouded Banes' weathered features. "Colter?"

"That's right," Colter said calmly. "I have some questions about a couple of men you might know."

Banes motioned to a chair across the table. "Marshal, pull up a chair. How 'bout somethin' to eat? I recommend the stew."

Colter ordered the stew and took a swallow of coffee,

leveling his eyes on Banes. "Do you know a lawman by the name of Farnsworth?"

Banes squirmed in his chair, avoided Colter's gaze, and looked out the window. "Farnsworth?" Banes picked at his teeth and contemplated. "No, don't believe I do."

"You don't remember talking to a big redheaded fella and a wagonload of prisoners? They got on your train at Omaha, the same one you rode, and got off at the end of track."

Banes felt Colter's hostility. There was no way out of this. He remembered the deep blue eyes of the prisoner called Colter. This Colter had those piercing blue eyes. There had to be a connection.

"Marshal, now that ya mention it, the wagon and all, I do remember talkin' to a fella like that." Banes' sweaty brow furrowed, and he added, "Not sure of his name, though. It coulda been Farnsworth."

"The name Gibbons mean anything to you?" Colter watched Banes and got the expected reaction.

"Nope. I've knowed some Gibbons along the way. Anythin' partic'lar 'bout this one?"

"Farnsworth and Gibbons may be one and the same."

Banes' mind was numbed. This Colter was onto something. How did he know about Farnsworth and the prisoners? It must have been that Wellsley girl who told him. Colter will want to go out to the end of track. Hackett had to clear out, and quick.

Banes tapped on the window and motioned to a seedy man. "Marshal, I'll be right back. Gotta tell one o' my men somethin'."

Colter had finished the stew when Banes returned. "One other thing, Banes. Have you seen a fella, not too tall but built like a tree, thick through the middle? Probably a muleskinner or a bullwhacker."

Banes shrugged. "Got a name? Out here that could fit a hun'erd men."

"Don't have a name, but he knows Farnsworth."

Banes' big hands nervously turned his coffee cup. "Sorry, Marshal, without a name I can't help ya. Why are ya lookin' for these men?"

"I'm guessing Farnsworth's real name is Gibbons. He's an army deserter. He and this other fella, I suspect, are holding prisoners who were smuggled from a Union prison camp. My father may be one of those prisoners."

Colter was too close. Sweat streamed rivulets down Banes' sides, and there was a growing knot in his belly. Most lawmen he knew could be intimidated or bought off, but Colter was not that kind. He was tough and, Banes suspected, honest. They would have to kill him to save their hides.

Banes leaned back in his chair. "I'm sorry 'bout your Pa. What makes ya think he's out this way?"

Colter steadily eyed Banes. "The trail leads this way."

Banes pushed back his chair. "I'll be leavin' shortly for the end of track. Ya wanna go?"

Colter nodded. "You're reading my mind, Banes."

Pug Hackett found the bottle Banes kept in a drawer. He leaned back in the chair, put his feet on the table, and took a long swallow from the bottle. Soon the whiskey would make him meaner than a sore-tailed cat. Hackett saw his means of income slipping away, and he didn't like Banes telling him what to do. He looked out the dirty window, took a drink, and belched. The approaching rider drove his horse at a frenzied pace, and then yanked his mount to a stop by Gibbons. They exchanged words, and then the rider kicked his horse to a hard gallop.

"Hackett!"

Cursing, Hackett threw open the door. An empty bottle dangled from his right hand. He stumbled down the steps, then swayed and squinted up at the rider. The drifter's beady eyes darted about as he wiped his sweaty, dust-covered face on a sleeve. The roan's frothy mouth and lathered withers indicated a spent mount.

Hackett sneered, "Yeah, what'cha want, Arneaux?"

Agitated, Arneaux blurted, "Banes said ya better git your men and clear out now. There's a Deputy United States Marshal Colter on his way out here."

Hackett cursed and threw the bottle against a wheel with such force that it shattered in small pieces that sparkled like diamonds.

"Colter?" Hackett slurred.

"Yeah, Colter." Arneaux hesitated, then leaned forward. "Banes said there's some connection between this Colter and one of your pris'ners."

Hackett paced and then scoffed. "He ain't a prisoner no more. Turned him loose up north."

"Hackett, this Marshal Colter ain't somebody to mess with. He and this other marshal went in the Last Chance askin' 'bout some jasper called Draik. Colter handled Big Ed Bigelow like a matchstick."

Hackett grunted and scowled at Arneaux. "Tell Gibbons to git the pris'ners ready to move out. Hurry!"

Gibbons was watching the prisoners while they shoveled and carted dirt and rock when Arneaux pulled up and leaned forward on the pommel. "Hackett said to git the pris'ners ready to pull out. There's trouble comin'."

Gibbons looked suspiciously at Arneaux. "What kinda trouble?"

"A Marshal Colter is headed this way, and he ain't somebody to mess with."

Gibbons' jaw dropped. "Ya say Colter?"

"Yep, and there's maybe a connection with one of your pris'ners."

Gibbons scurried to round up the prisoners and then herded them to the wagon. After locking them up, he hitched the team of mules as Hackett weaved his way to the wagon.

"Pug, what are we gonna do?" Gibbons asked fearfully.

Hackett growled, "Git a holt yo'self, Gibbons. We'll find cover at Lodgepole Crick and hide 'til dark. Then we'll take care o' that Marshal Colter and head for the Black Hills and dig some coal."

"Come on, Banes," Colter urged impatiently under his breath.

"Marshal," Banes said, waving a hand. "I gotta stop by the Union Pacific before we go."

Colter figured that Banes was stalling for time. But why? Did he send that drifter out to the end of track to warn someone?

Colter was edgy when Banes reappeared, wiping his face with a red bandanna. "Be with ya in a minute, Marshal. Got to git my horse from the liv'ry."

"Better hurry, Banes. I'm leaving with or without you."

Colter swung into the saddle and headed for the end of track. Banes caught up, astride a sorrel with white stocking feet. Colter turned Smoke, making sure Banes didn't get behind him.

"Hold it, Marshal. My horse done picked up a stone or somethin'."

Colter reined in as Banes slipped from the saddle and looked at the sorrel's right front hoof.

Banes said, "Figgered it'd be a stone."

While Banes removed the stone, Colter considered the

possibility that Banes had planted the stone in the sorrel's hoof to buy time.

Colter grew restless. "Banes, I want to get there before dark."

An hour of daylight remained when they drew up at the end of track. The construction site reminded Colter of a bed of ants. He guessed there were seventy-five men at the site, many of them Chinese. The ping of hammer and spike set a rhythm as some swung picks while others shoveled dirt and rock into wagons and wheelbarrows. He didn't see a wagon that fit the description of the one Ellen had seen.

Banes smiled assertively and pointed to the only car at the site. "Marshal, look around. I'll be in my office over there."

Colter swung down from the saddle and wandered among the workers. The Chinese worked as a group, while others were spread over the site. Many of these men were running from something, usually the law, but some were good people with families. No one knew anything about Gibbons or Farnsworth or a wagon and prisoners. Colter was disappointed, but not surprised. Some didn't like the law asking questions, and others didn't want to jeopardize their jobs. Banes' man had done the job. Gibbons had cleared out.

Colter mounted and then he heard, "Marshal Colter."

He turned and saw Banes standing in the doorway of the coachlike car. He nudged Smoke in that direction.

The cocksure Banes hooked a thumb in his belt and drew on a cigar. "Marshal, General Grenville Dodge will be arrivin' tomorrow to inspect our progress. Why don't ya stay and meet him?"

Colter wheeled his mount, saying, "I'll do that if I'm around."

Colter swung wide of the site, searching for the one set of wagon tracks that would lead him to Gibbons and the prisoners. His heartbeat quickened. They had been here. Gibbons, he figured, would have gone toward Lodgepole Creek.

Colter crisscrossed the terrain, and as dusk neared he spotted the tracks. He saw a distant flash of lightning, heard the roll of thunder, and felt the cool west wind as he eased off Smoke. If it rained, the tracks would be difficult to follow. Then his only hope would be to spot a campfire.

Colter knelt to inspect the tracks for any distinguishing marks, like a cracked rim. After following the tracks, it became obvious that the wagon went over a ridge, and he guessed Lodgepole Creek would be on the other side.

Colter stepped into the saddle. He would skirt around the crest of the ridge and pick up the tracks on the other side. A glance to the west told him he would have to hurry. The approaching darkness and rain-laden clouds posed a threat to tracking Gibbons.

He rounded the ridge and saw Lodgepole Creek, lined with cottonwoods and a dense stand of willows. Colter scanned the creek for movement and then picked up the tracks at the base of the ridge. He didn't like it. With no cover, he was an easy target.

Colter slouched low in the saddle when a jagged streak of lightning pierced the ground nearby, followed by a deafening peal of thunder. Smoke reared, and Colter grabbed the pommel to keep from being unseated. He was fighting to control Smoke when his head seemed to explode. Colter slumped forward and slid out of the saddle, landing in the prairie dust where muted raindrops gathered intensity.

Chapter Ten

Jed Colter lay in the prairie mud, wincing at the throb in his head. The thunderstorm had swept across the plains, leaving a chill and puddles of water. He shivered, turned on his back, and saw the moon under a canopy of stars. After struggling to a sitting position, he wiped mud from his face and gingerly examined the furrowlike crease above his left ear.

Judging from the moon's position, Colter guessed it was an hour until dawn. He got to a knee and waited for the dizziness to pass. After finding his hat, he gently placed it on his head. A nearby soft whinny brought comfort.

"Come here, Smoke."

Hesitantly, Smoke approached Colter. "Good boy."

Colter reached into a pocket for sugar but didn't find any. He grabbed the reins and wrangled Smoke closer. Colter pulled himself up by a stirrup and leaned against Smoke until the spinning subsided. He crawled into the saddle and leaned over the withers as his belly churned.

Colter nudged Smoke toward Lodgepole Creek. He figured the bushwhacker was Gibbons or Hackett. Or maybe it was somebody Banes had sent. Whoever it was, they likely thought he was dead and that was to his advantage. Nearing the willows, he eased out his Colt and slipped from the saddle. Colter crouched low as he moved stealthily through the willows. Abruptly, he broke out into a small clearing and pulled back. Colter scanned the surroundings before crossing the clearing. He carefully groped through the willows until he reached Lodgepole Creek. A trickle of water threaded its way through the grassy creek bed. Cottonwoods on the opposite bank partially obscured his vision beyond. Colter stepped over the small stream and worked his way through the cottonwoods to the open prairie. A look upstream and then downstream didn't show any sign of anyone being there.

Colter retraced his steps across Lodgepole Creek. Smoke had wandered, nibbling at bunchgrass. Colter took the trailing reins and moved to the creek bed, where he found a spot in the midst of a thick clump of willows under a cottonwood with low-hanging limbs. He built a fire using dry leaves from the hollow of a cottonwood. The spiral of smoke was dispersed through the cottonwood limbs, making it difficult to see from a distance.

A nearby pool provided water for coffee. The eastern horizon had given way to a fiery golden hue while Colter surveyed his condition. His clothing and boots were caked with mud.

Colter checked the coffee and figured he had time to clean his wound. After washing his face, he soaked a faded red bandanna and swabbed the furrow above his left ear. When he had finished, Colter rinsed the bandanna and tied it around his head.

Two prairie dogs playfully scampered about, barking

and darting in and out of holes as Colter returned to the fire. After his fill of coffee, jerky, and biscuits, Colter knelt by the pool. The camp was well concealed, but the pool was exposed to the open prairie.

Colter removed his vest and shirt, exposing a lean and hard upper body that rippled with each movement. As he dipped and scrubbed the shirt, his eyes moved continuously over the prairie. Movement upstream caught his eye. Colter grew angry with himself for leaving the Henry in the scabbard. When three pronghorns broke out into the clearing, he relaxed with a sigh. After cleaning his pants, Colter finished dressing, doused the fire with the remaining coffee, then scattered the coals.

Colter pulled into the saddle and crossed Lodgepole Creek, where he searched for wagon tracks. He closely checked upstream and downstream, but found no sign. The rain had filled the tracks. Colter could only guess the direction Gibbons had taken. After an hour of searching, he broke it off, when the plaintive signal of a train wafted across the plains. He remembered Banes telling him that General Dodge would be arriving today. Disappointed, Colter turned Smoke and headed for the end of track.

Three young Arapaho braves found him crouched among the willows along Lodgepole Creek. He had tried to run from them, but his strength betrayed him. It had been days since he had anything to eat, except for a few grasshoppers and a little grass. Jim Colter watched the bucks move around him, their curiosity piqued. Where was he? Why was he here? How did he get here? His name, he couldn't remember. He was in trouble and couldn't defend himself. They taunted him in a language he didn't understand. The Colter fire burned within, but all he could do was try to avoid their rushes. Each brave took a turn charging at him, leaning far to the side of his pony and reaching out as he passed Colter to touch him or grab his hair or beard.

Jim Colter had survived the war, prison camp, a mine cave-in, and Pug Hackett's whip and fists. A man of dignity and discipline, his forty-six years and a hard life had brought a stoop to his shoulders. Standing six feet, he had the competitive spirit and handsome features possessed by all the Colter men.

He watched as the Indians circled him on their ponies. Their bronze bodies were lean and hard. From their actions, he figured they were tiring of playing with him. The cat and mouse game was over. Curious prairie dogs had ducked back into the safety of their holes. He looked around for something to use as a weapon, but there was nothing. Jim Colter stood proud and defiantly. If they were going to finish the job, he would make at least one of them remember this day.

The braves yelped and shouted, feeling confident and ready for the kill. One of them broke off from the others, turned his pony toward Colter, and began the charge. Colter knelt on one knee and intently watched the onrushing Indian. On previous passes, he had ducked to avoid the Indian's grasp. This time, he waited until the buck leaned over for his grab. Colter came to a crouch and put his elbow and shoulder into the Indian's face. The brave's eyes widened in disbelief as Colter's elbow crushed his nose and sent him tumbling like a rag doll into the prairie dust, where he lay motionless.

Jim Colter felt a sense of victory and rubbed his numbed elbow. One of the remaining braves eased his pony over to the downed Indian. After a close look, he wheeled his pony, and with a guttural scream, charged. Jim Colter was spent.

He sidestepped the rush, but it was too late. The pony's shoulder sent him sprawling into a patch of sagebrush. He heard a crack, like a gunshot, and the world spun crazily as he fought desperately to regain his senses. The ground shook with the rumble of hooves. The yaps and yelps of the Indians seemed so distant.

Jed Colter felt the chill sweeping across the plains. It was the first of many that told of the coming of fall. The days were losing the intense heat of the plains sun; the nights were colder. He had felt the sting of the norther down in Texas. Here, with the ever present wind, the sting would last for months.

The hiss of steam and the ping of hammers signaled the end of track as he topped the rise. Colter drew up next to a wagon with a broken wheel and eased out of the saddle. The exertion made him dizzy. Pausing, he looked over the frenzied activity and was amazed at the progress since the day before. He spotted what he figured was General Dodge's car and headed in that direction.

"Marshal." Colter heard the muffled voice, glanced around, but didn't see anyone.

"Marshal Colter!"

Colter measuredly looked around and saw a man crouched between two boxcars, motioning for him. The man peeked around the corner of the car as Colter joined him.

"Marshal, I'm Ned O'Quinn," he said, extending his hand.

O'Quinn had the look of the Irish. A head shorter than Colter, his square jaw and thick neck joined a barrel chest, short waist, and bowed legs. Dark, curly hair topped a face sun-scorched to a dark brown. Colter felt the strength in O'Quinn's large hamlike hand and detected a slight Irish brogue.

"Mr. O'Quinn, what can you tell me about what's going on here?"

O'Quinn's eyes darted about. Colter's pulse quickened.

"Marshal, if Banes finds out I talked to you, he'll kill me."

"You won't have to worry about Banes."

O'Quinn peeked around the corner and looked up at Colter.

"I been wantin' to tell somebody 'bout this for a long time. In fact, ever since that Hackett showed up with them prisoners 'bout a year ago."

Colter grew intense. "Hackett?"

O'Quinn blinked and shuffled his feet. "Yeah, Pug Hackett and that Farnsworth fella. I've heard Hackett call him Gibbons."

"This Farnsworth. Big redheaded, red-faced fella missing his left earlobe?"

O'Quinn nodded. "Yeah that's him!"

"I believe his name is Gibbons. The other fella, Hackett. Short, built like a tree trunk?"

"That's him. Meaner than a snake. Carries a whip." O'Quinn grimaced and shook his head. "I've seen him hit some of them prisoners so hard I thought it would break their neck, and they was in shackles."

Colter felt the knot in his belly and asked, "What can you tell me about the prisoners?"

"Up 'til two days ago there was four."

"Four? What happened?" Colter asked anxiously.

"I don't rightly know. Probably same thing that happened to that poor Lemmon."

"Who's Lemmon?" Colter asked, remembering Ebetts calling one of the prisoners Lemmon.

"Jake Lemmon. He was one of Hackett's prisoners. From all accounts, Lemmon was givin' Hackett trouble, and then one day Lemmon is missin' and we don't see him again. I figger Hackett took him out away from the tracks and killed him."

"You know the names of the other prisoners?"

O'Quinn looked around the corner of the car. He pulled back, took out a blue bandanna, and wiped his face.

"Marshal, that Gibbons wouldn't let nobody talk to them prisoners, but I heard him call out their names." O'Quinn paused, thought a moment, and continued, "One of them fellas he called Cain. Don't know his first name. Then there's the Acker boy. I believe his name is Matt. The other one is Buck Trendell."

Colter grimaced as the knot in his belly grew larger.

"Who's the other one?"

O'Quinn's eyes met Colter's and neither blinked.

"Marshal, would you be kin of Jim Colter?"

Jed Colter felt a chill. "My father. What's happened?"

"I knowed it, Marshal. It's the eyes." O'Quinn grinned, and then grew somber. "I don't know what's happened to Mr. Colter. A few days back, Banes went out to see the prisoners with this Hackett fella. But somethin' happened before that to Mr. Colter. I didn't see him for two days. That's not unusual, since it took two days for 'em to recover from one of Hackett's beatin's. Then Mr. Colter showed back up, but he wasn't the same. He seemed confused. Didn't appear to know where he was and moved real slow. I figger Hackett beat him. Then two, three days ago, he disappears again and I ain't seen him since."

"Did you see Hackett and Gibbons leave with the prisoners?"

O'Quinn nodded. "Yesterday, before you come out, this Arneaux fella high-tailed it out here and told Hackett to clear out quick. Hackett and Gibbons rounded up the prisoners and took off towards Lodgepole Creek." He gestured to the bandanna on Colter's head. "Did you have a run-in with 'em, Marshal?"

"Somebody bushwhacked me at Lodgepole Creek. I figure it was them. Any idea where they were headed?"

With a lift of his chin, O'Quinn indicated west. "My guess is that Banes sent 'em up in the Black Hills to dig coal. Banes told me some time back there was a good deposit of coal over there and the Union Pacific would be needin' it."

"Do you know what kind of arrangement Banes has with Hackett?"

O'Quinn pushed back his hat and hooked a thumb in his suspenders.

"Well, Marshal, I been studyin' on that. I figger Banes is in thick with Hackett. I don't know for sure, but I calc'late the Union Pacific is payin' full labor for each prisoner. Banes is takin' his cut and givin' the rest to Hackett."

"Mr. O'Quinn, you've cleared up a lot of things. Don't worry about Banes. He'll be taken care of after I talk to General Dodge." Colter turned to go, and then asked, "Any idea what Hackett might have done with my father?"

"Marshal, I hate to think about it. In his condition, Mr. Colter was of no use to Hackett. I figger he took Mr. Colter out a ways and left him. Hackett is the devil hisself." O'Quinn shook his head. "I just don't want to think about it."

O'Quinn's words were clear. Colter felt the emptiness in his belly that always seemed to come when he got so close and failed. Where would he start looking on this endless prairie?

Colter left O'Quinn and crossed over the tracks to Dodge's coach. He pulled up on the first step as Harley Banes opened the door.

Banes smiled. "Marshal, I'm glad ya was able to make it back."

"Yeah, I bet you are, Banes," Colter snapped and stepped down. "You have any idea who would ambush me over at Lodgepole Creek?"

Banes frowned as he stepped to the ground. "Ambushed ya? What'cha mean, Marshal? You're not accusin' me, are ya?"

"No, I'm accusing Hackett and Gibbons. They're friends of yours, aren't they?"

Banes feigned innocence. "Marshal, I don't know no Hackett or Gibbons. What's this all about?"

Colter prodded, "You're lying, Banes. I know about the prisoners, and that at least one is dead and maybe another. I know about your deal with Hackett, and that makes you just as guilty as Hackett of Jake Lemmon's death."

Banes began to sweat copiously. "Colter, I don't know what'cha talkin' 'bout, and who is this Lemmon?"

Colter glared and took a menacing step toward Banes. Panic boiled in Banes' belly as he turned Colter's accusations over in his mind. The marshal was right, but where had he gotten his information?

"Banes, one of those prisoners is my father, and I understand he's disappeared. Is he dead?"

Banes's mind couldn't function fast enough and perspiration streamed from his armpits. No man had buffaloed him like this Colter. He couldn't match Colter in a gunfight, but the marshal was not himself with that head wound. Maybe he could get the best of Colter with his fists. After all, he had taken out a few men in his time. He spotted Arneaux over Colter's right shoulder, slowly moving toward them. A sense of confidence returned. Arneaux gripped a shovel and was poised to strike. Banes shuffled his feet and stepped back to cover Arneaux's approach.

Banes smirked, "Colter, I ain't done nothin', and I ain't tellin' ya nothin'."

Anger seized Colter as he took a step toward Banes. He heard a grunt, then felt the blow to his head. His knees buckled, and he lost consciousness.

"Arneaux, ya didn't git here any too soon. I thought I was a goner." Banes looked down at Colter and added, "The marshal knows everythin' but what happ'ned to his pa. Soon as I finish him, we gotta high-tail it outta here."

Banes reached for the Colt on his right hip.

"Now, Marshal, I have the upper hand."

He brought the gun in line with Colter's chest and smiled as he gently squeezed the trigger.

Chapter Eleven

The din of hoofbeats ceased, an eerie silence masking the prairie. A distant rumble grew into hoofbeats. Why did the Indians leave, and why were they returning? Jim Colter lay still, reluctant to open his eyes. The pungent aroma of the sagebrush was heavy in his nostrils. There was a presence. A shadow crossed over him, and he felt a hand on his shoulder.

"Mister, you all right?"

Colter warily opened his eyes to see an Indian kneeling by him. He drew back and saw a second Indian. It wasn't the two bucks who tried to kill him. These were dressed differently.

"I Little Raven, that Johnny Hawk," Raven said as he nodded in Hawk's direction.

Little Raven continued, "We Pawnee soldiers. We saw what happen, chase off Arapaho. You brave man. What you doin' out here? Who are you?"

A bewildered Jim Colter stared at Little Raven, then

shifted his gaze to Hawk. He was at a loss for words and didn't know his name.

Hawk tapped a forefinger on his head and said, "Evil spirits."

Little Raven moved when Colter sat upright. Evil spirits or not, they couldn't leave him out here.

Little Raven squinted up at Hawk. "He hungry. Get jerky and hardtack."

Hawk removed a cloth sack from his saddle and passed it to an eager Colter.

Little Raven motioned to Hawk. "Water."

Hawk backed away, holding up his hands. "No. No water. Evil spirits."

Little Raven said impatiently, "My canteen."

Hawk reluctantly brought Little Raven's canteen and held it out to Colter.

After finishing the jerky and hardtack, Colter took long swallows of water.

Colter skewed his eyes up at the Pawnees. "Sam. Sam's the name. Thank you for saving my life."

He got to a knee, gathered himself, and rose to his feet. While flexing an aching arm and massaging his right shoulder, Colter checked the surroundings and then passed the canteen to Little Raven.

"Where are we?" Colter asked.

Little Raven pointed north and said, "Hour's ride from John Leach's ranch. We take you there. Leach good man. He take care of you."

As Colter spoke, Hawk lost his fear of evil spirits. Hawk's gaze met the penetrating eyes of Jim Colter. He blinked and was taken aback. Those eyes. He had seen eyes like Sam's. And he had heard that voice.

"Sam, ride with me," Little Raven said as he took the reins and mounted. He reached down and pulled Colter up behind him. Their ponies shied away from the dead body of the Arapaho.

Soft hoofbeats and the creaking of leather broke the prairie silence. Hawk caught Little Raven's attention, lowered his right shoulder, and swung his elbow around.

"Like to see face of Arapaho when he saw Sam's elbow."

Hawk's eyes flared open with a slack jaw. They laughed heartily. Jim Colter smiled.

Harley Banes heard the rifle crack as his Colt roared and bucked against his palm. Something tugged at his sleeve, throwing off his aim. His bullet dug into the ground near Jed Colter's head.

Arneaux shouted, "It's one o' them Pawnee soldiers! Let's git outta here!"

Banes cursed and wheeled about as another bullet passed his ear. He snapped a shot at the Pawnee kneeling by Dodge's coach.

Arneaux had scrambled to a horse and pulled into the saddle. Banes grimaced and hurriedly fired at Colter. The bullet plowed up dirt to Colter's left as the Pawnee leveled his rifle at Banes and squeezed off another shot. Banes turned and stumbled, feeling the bullet's breeze under his chin. Regaining his balance, Banes raced for the mount Arneaux held for him. Clawing at the pommel, he jerked into the saddle and dug his heels into the horse. Banes and Arneaux frantically left the end of track as curious eyes followed them until they disappeared over a rise.

Banes busily thought about his next move. He and Arneaux would split up in Cheyenne. Then he would lay low until he could figure a way to get Colter. It wouldn't be easy to find a place where he could keep an eye out for where Colter was and follow his movements. Lodgepole! He had been to the Westerner's Saloon in Lodgepole. There were rooms upstairs where he could hole up, and Colter and that sheriff would never know until it was too late. Pulling ahead of Arneaux, he smiled at his ingenious idea.

"Harley!"

Banes was yanked from his thoughts by Arneaux's frenzied shout. He turned in the saddle to see Arneaux hysterically kicking the sides of his mount and using the quirt. Banes spotted the reason for Arneaux's concern. Indians! Five of them. While in thought, he had forgotten the threat of Indians.

Banes leaned over the withers, looked around, and saw Arneaux was losing ground.

"Better him than me. Maybe they'll be satisfied with one scalp."

He used the quirt and heard a distant cry of agony. Banes glanced over his shoulder. The Indians converged on Arneaux like a pack of wolves. The yelping, yapping, and screams faded. Banes topped a ridge and looked back. The Indians had broken off the chase. When Cheyenne was in sight, Banes eased up. He checked his mount and shuddered. In their haste to leave the end of track, he had mounted Arneaux's jaded horse. Still, it was faster than his sorrel.

Banes squirmed at the thought of having Colter on his trail. There was no quit in the man. It was like Colter had a veil of protection around him. Banes cursed and swore to finish the job Hackett and Gibbons couldn't do.

Ned O'Quinn heard the gunshots, but that was not unusual since the Pawnee soldiers often fired at coyotes and prairie dogs. His brow wrinkled when he saw Banes and

Arneaux scurry from the end of track. Did Colter tell Dodge about Banes and his arrangement with Hackett? If so, Dodge would have fired Banes. The general didn't tolerate such things. Why hadn't Colter stopped Banes? Colter knew enough about Banes to put a noose around his neck. Then it hit him. The gunshots! Maybe Banes and Arneaux had gotten the drop on them.

O'Quinn ran to Dodge's car. Had Banes and Arneaux killed Colter? Or maybe the general? He rounded the coach and saw a Pawnee soldier kneeling by Colter.

O'Quinn shouted, "Marshal! What happened? Is Gen'ral Dodge all right?"

"I," the Pawnee soldier said, "Runs-With-Antelope. I save Colter. That fella, Banes, try to kill Colter. I shoot, scare off Banes."

O'Quinn started to speak, but the Pawnee abruptly turned and went back to his post. Colter held his head between his hands, wobbling. O'Quinn helped him to a knee.

The door of Dodge's coach swung open.

"What in blazes is going on out there? You men take your fight someplace else."

Dodge spoke around a cigar that punctuated his bearded, neatly trimmed face. He glared at O'Quinn and tugged on a sleeve of his uniform.

O'Quinn looked up, gasping for air.

"No, Gen'ral sir, we're not fightin'. This here's Marshal Colter. He's here 'bout Banes."

"Banes?" Dodge asked. He flicked the cigar ash and then continued. "What about Banes?"

"It's a long story, Gen'ral."

Dodge leaned over Colter and said, "Good heavens, man, let's get him inside."

Together, Dodge and O'Quinn pulled Colter to his feet.

In Dodge's private coach, they stretched Colter out on a cot used by the general's servant—a lean, rangy black man.

Dodge snapped his fingers. "Mose, get a washcloth for the marshal."

Mose applied the damp cloth to Colter's forehead and jumped back as Colter bolted upright.

"Where's Banes?"

O'Quinn had his wind back and put a hand on Colter's shoulder.

"Easy, Marshal. Him and that Arneaux fella lit out real fast. I heard gunshots and suspected somethin' was wrong, so I come up to see what might make them two high-tail it out like they did. That's when I found you on the ground. Banes tried to kill you, but one of the Pawnees saved your goose."

"Which Pawnee?" Colter asked.

"Calls hisself Runs-with-Antelope."

Colter looked up at the man in uniform.

"Sir, you must be General Dodge."

"That I am, Marshal," Dodge said, blowing a cloud of smoke.

Colter extended a hand. "Forgive me, General, for not getting up. I'm Deputy United States Marshal Jed Colter. I had the pleasure of meeting you when you visited West Point in '61."

Dodge took Colter's hand, and with a note of surprise, asked, "You were at West Point in '61?"

"Yes, sir. I resigned in May of '61 under honorable circumstances."

"To join the war I presume?"

"No, sir, I came west. I couldn't fight against family or friend."

"I must say I'm disappointed you didn't take a stand and

commit to one side or the other. A fella has just got to stand up and fight for what he believes." Dodge contemplated and shook his head. "It must have been a difficult decision. There was so much turmoil at the Point back then. So many young men died; so many careers ended prematurely."

"Sir, I made a decision that I thought was best for me. Maybe that was wrong, but that's the position I took and I'll stand by it."

The general nodded and said, "I respect your honesty, Marshal." Dodge turned to O'Quinn and continued, "Now, sir, who are you?"

"Sir, I'm Ned O'Quinn. I'm in charge of the graders."

Dodge grunted and removed the cigar. "And a fine job you're doing, O'Quinn. Now what's this about Banes?"

Colter told Dodge about Banes and his connection with Hackett and Gibbons. The general shook his head in disbelief as Colter unfolded the facts.

"Banes was a good man, Marshal," Dodge said, pacing the length of the room. "I can't believe he would do something like this."

Disappointment was evident in Dodge's voice, like a father who learns his son is a thief.

Colter nodded at O'Quinn. "I had some of it figured out, but Mr. O'Quinn pieced it all together."

Dodge waved an arm in a sweeping motion toward the vast prairie.

"And your father may be out there somewhere."

"Yes, sir, and hopefully still alive."

"Marshal Colter, I feel some responsibility here. I can't fathom this happening without me knowing it." The general paced, then continued, "O'Quinn, I want you to take as many men as you feel necessary and go look for the marshal's father. He can't be too far out, so confine your search to a reasonable distance from here."

"Yes, sir."

Dodge held up his right hand. "And one other thing, O'Quinn. What is your background here?"

O'Quinn grinned. "Well, sir, I've been a track layer, surveyor, grader, built bridges, and used pick and shovel."

Dodge hesitated and then made his decision. "Mr. O'Quinn, you're taking Banes' place. Tell the foremen to come up here. They need to know what's going on. Then get some men together and start the search."

"Thank you, Gen'ral. I'll get started right away."

Dodge wanted to beat the Central Pacific over the mountains. Colter realized what a sacrifice it was for the general to take that many men off the job to look for his father.

"General, I'm very grateful for your offer."

"Think nothing of it, Marshal. You need to rest here a while until you can get back on your feet."

"Thank you, sir."

Dodge reached for the door to his quarters. He paused and said amid a cloud of cigar smoke, "Mose, see that the marshal gets what he needs."

Mose nodded, "Yes, sir."

Colter hadn't noticed the plush surroundings until he lay back on the cot. The general's quarters were to the rear of the car, separated by a mahogany-paneled wall. A door with a gold-plated knob stood slightly ajar. Lace-covered windows were adorned with burgundy velvet curtains, tied back by gold-colored braided rope.

Time was precious, so he couldn't stay here long. Colter felt a hand on his shoulder.

"The gen'ral say it ain't no good to sleep so soon after a knock on the head like you got."

Colter looked up at Mose. His was a gentle face, crowned with a hoary thatch.

"Thanks, Mose."

Colter swung his legs over the side of the cot and massaged the lump on the back of his head. The throb he expected didn't come until he stood up. He put out a hand to steady himself while Mose took the other arm until he was sure Colter could stand on his own.

"Can I git you anything else, Marshal?"

"I'd like some water." Colter rubbed the back of his head, then continued, "Is the general in his quarters?"

"Yes, Marshal. G'on in, he won't mind." Mose leaned close to Colter and whispered, "Marshal, the gen'ral was kinda hard on you 'bout the war and all. Don't take it too hard. I can tell when he likes somebody, and he likes you."

Colter took the water from Mose, drank it, and eased through the door after knocking. Dodge sat behind a mahogany desk. Papers and pencils were organized neatly on the desk. A sofa, chair, and table with a lamp evened out the general's office. A photograph of Dodge, Grant, Sheridan, and Sherman hung on the wall behind the general. Polished brass handrails ran the length of each wall.

Dodge looked up from his desk. "Feeling better, Marshal?"

"Somewhat, General. I'm leaving for Cheyenne. Thank you, sir, for all you've done."

"Marshal, I wish you would spend the night. You need the rest, and we could talk about the Point."

"I'd like that, sir, but I must pick up Banes' trail."

Dodge got up, extending a hand. "Good luck, Marshal." Their eyes held for a moment. He turned, then paused, looking back at Colter with a smile. "I hope we meet again. I can always use good men like you."

"Thank you, sir. I'll keep that in mind."

Dodge watched Colter leave and speculated that he would have made a fine officer. Dodge smiled and had a feeling he had not heard the last of Jed Colter.

Colter eased into the saddle, searching for the Pawnee soldier. He spotted a Pawnee and nudged Smoke ahead.

He pulled up by the Pawnee and said, "I'm looking for Runs-with-Antelope."

The Pawnee, slight of build, looked up at Colter and brought a fist to his chest. "I, Runs-with-Antelope."

Colter dismounted and stuck out a hand. "I want to thank you for saving my life."

Runs-with-Antelope hesitated and then took Colter's hand. His aquiline nose flared. Suddenly the stoic face broke into a smile.

"Can't wait to tell Johnny Hawk I save Colter's life."

Colter laughed and said, "When you see Johnny Hawk and Little Raven, tell them I said hello."

Runs-with-Antelope nodded, then Colter pulled into the saddle.

Colter figured there were three hours of daylight remaining when he left the end of track. Smoke's rhythmic stride agitated the throb in his head. He approached each rise cautiously and scanned the horizon in every direction. Two hours from Cheyenne, he saw vultures circling over the next rise. He reached for the Henry while his heart pounded. Was it his father? A man in his condition couldn't survive out here. There was no water, except after a rain, and then it quickly disappeared. Without a gun, food was almost impossible to come by. The nights were getting colder.

Colter nudged Smoke ahead and drew up when he rounded the rise. Staying below the crest, he scanned the ambient terrain, watching for movement. The Indian could fade into the environment like a chameleon. Colter's eyes moved to the circling vultures and attempted to pick up the object of their attention. He moved the grulla ahead at a canter, keeping his eyes peeled. A sick feeling churned in his belly.

"Easy now."

Now the vultures were overhead. Colter pulled up when he saw a vulture on the ground near an object. It was an animal or the body of a man.

The immediate terrain was shaped like a bowl with a dimpled bottom. Sparse prickly pear and sagebrush splattered across the landscape. Colter wiped sweat from his brow and eased Smoke closer. The vulture flapped its wings, squawked, and flew off to a safe distance. Smoke grew skittish as they approached what Colter now knew was the body of a man. He dropped to the ground and examined the unshod tracks of several horses. Uncertainty hounded Colter. He was exposed without the protection of a tree or boulder. Was he set up for another ambush? He moved forward, clutching the Henry in his right hand and the reins in his left.

Colter knelt by the body. His head throbbed with anticipation as he turned it over. It was not his father. He paused, fighting back tears of relief. Arapaho arrows protruded from the rib cage and belly. The scalped man was not Banes. Could he be the man who was traveling with Banes? O'Quinn had called him Arneaux. There was some familiarity about him. What about Banes? Did they get him too?

Fearing Smoke would likely bolt at the scent of blood, Colter kept him on a tight rein, upwind of the body. Colter placed the stranger across the grulla's rump and secured it with a piggin' string. Leaning over to check the cinches, he heard the swish, the thud, and the quiver of an arrow as it ripped into the left thigh of the stranger. Colter spun around, frantically searching for the attacker. An Arapaho buck some fifty feet away struggled to ready another arrow for delivery. Colter was reluctant to use his Henry. That would alert others in the area. How did he miss the Arapaho? This one had stayed behind, hoping to add a scalp to his collection. Maybe his first.

Colter's mind raced. He had to avoid the next arrow and rush the brave before he could ready another arrow. Intently watching the Indian rise up and take aim, Colter timed his lunge as the arrow cut air. The arrow swished by and plowed into the ground behind Colter. He rolled over, got to his feet, and sprinted as gracefully as a big cat toward the startled Indian, quickly closing the distance. The buck turned and ran but Colter was on him, swinging the Henry like an ax. The brave crumpled after Colter clubbed him on the head. Colter knelt by the Arapaho.

"You won't be giving anybody any trouble for a while." Colter looked around for Smoke, then continued, "That is, if we can get out of here in a hurry."

Colter scanned the horizon for visitors and then located Smoke. The horse was restive and shied away as Colter approached. After coaxing Smoke, Colter moved close enough to grab the reins. He removed the arrow from the stranger and tugged on the cinches. Colter jammed the Henry in the scabbard, climbed into the saddle, and turned toward Cheyenne.

Colter checked his back trail often. Dusk had gathered when he pulled up at the U.S. Marshal's office in Cheyenne. Red Ilsen bounded out the door to meet him.

"You get Draik?" Ilsen asked hopefully.

Colter eased from the saddle and said, "No, this stranger's luck ran out when he got caught by the Arapaho."

"Too bad, Jed. Word from Lodgepole is that Draik gunned down Sheriff Radison."

Colter wheeled, anger flushing his face. "Dead?"

"Last I heard he was hangin' on."

Colter realized Draik was playing a cat and mouse game with him. How did Draik know he was in these parts? Was Draik using Radison to get to him?

A crowd had gathered to gawk at the stranger's body. Murmurs and gasps emoted when they saw the missing scalp.

"Ever see him?" Colter asked Ilsen.

Ilsen nodded. "Around, but I don't know him."

Colter wiped a sleeve across his brow and said, "You see anything while I was gone?"

"No. Been keeping an eye on the Last Chance, but it's been quiet." He grinned. "I think you got their attention."

Colter asked, "You know Harley Banes?"

"Know of him. Why?"

"He's in cahoots with two other fellas, Hackett and Gibbons. If the Arapaho didn't get him, he's got to be in Cheyenne."

Colter told Ilsen about Banes and his arrangement with Hackett and Gibbons and what had happened at the end of track.

Ilsen pushed back his hat. "If he's here, we'll find him."

Colter was weary to the bone. He nodded toward the Union Pacific office and said, "Red, would you bring Mr. Weems here? He might know this man."

Ilsen was gone less than a minute when a pencil-thin man with a derby hat stepped through the crowd. "Need me to take that body, Marshal?"

"Soon as we get Mr. Weems to take a look. Who are you?"

"Koon," he said, dryly. "I'm the undertaker here."

Colter nodded. "Soon as someone can identify the body."

Ilsen returned with Weems, and Colter asked, "Mr. Weems, do you know this man?"

Weems flinched, and then stepped forward for a closer look.

The pasty-faced Weems swallowed. "Arneaux. He's one of Banes' men."

Colter asked expectantly, "Have you seen Banes?"

Weems wagged his head. "Not since you and him rode out to the end of track."

Disappointment cloaked Colter's face. "Thank you, Mr. Weems."

Colter looked at Koon and said, "You can take the body now."

He turned to Ilsen. "Red, let's go find Banes."

Chapter Twelve

A city of tents sprawled across the landscape, providing a home to tie hackers and coal diggers. Pug Hackett found it to his liking, his kind of people. A rectangular tent housed a makeshift bar consisting of two parallel boards supported by a barrel at each end. Tie hackers and coal diggers occupied randomly spaced tables. Cigarettes and cuds of tobacco littered the dirt floor. Wind groaned dolefully through the pines. Hackett pulled up the collar around his ears, fanned the cards, and suppressed a smile. The droopy-eyed fellow had dealt him a winning hand. The man's shaggy, straw-colored hair hung to the shoulder, and sun-bleached eyebrows twitched over wide-set eyes. Hackett hated snakes, and this one reminded him of the slithery reptile.

Hackett and Gibbons had joined Draik and settled in a camp of tie hackers and coal diggers high in the Black Hills of Wyoming, where the wind cut like a knife. When not cutting crossties or digging coal, they were usually here, swilling cheap whiskey and gambling away their wages. Remnants of a light snow remained. Conditions indicated there was more to come. Gibbons had taken the prisoners to an abandoned mine.

"Ya gonna hold 'em, Hackett?" Draik drawled.

"Yeah, Draik." Hackett smirked.

Draik took three cards and leaned back in his chair to study the hand he had dealt. A quirly dangled from a corner of his small mouth. A single rope of smoke curled upward until it was caught in a breeze and drifted into the gray haze overhead. Draik's long, slender fingers splayed his cards. He leaned forward, placing his elbows on the table. The droopy eyes locked on Hackett while he fondled a stack of gold coins.

"Gonna cost ya, Hackett, to stay in this game," Draik challenged, tossing five gold coins on the table.

Hackett laughed and wheezed. His tobacco-stained teeth clenched the cigar stub, squeezing a trickle of tobacco juice through the stubble and down his chin.

Hackett threw a gold eagle on the growing pot.

"Raise ya five."

Draik matched Hackett and spread his hand on the table with a cocked smile. He glared at Hackett while tapping a finger by his cards. Three jacks.

Hackett laughed, and Draik knew he had lost again. The thin face flushed and his eyes narrowed when Hackett displayed a straight flush. Draik's right hand moved unobtrusively to his gun. He never claimed to be good at cards, but he did win now and then. Tonight, he had not won a hand. Draik wondered about Hackett, but he had not seen him cheating.

Hackett reached for the pot, then looked up at Draik. "Tell ya what. Let me buy ya a drink."

Draik relaxed and moved his hand to the table when Hackett called for a bottle. Hackett's gaze swung around the tent. His beady eyes gleamed as he watched a young woman cavort with a tie hacker.

Hackett grinned and said, "Draik, ya need one them wenches. They'll calm your frustrations."

Draik's icy gaze leveled on Hackett. "I ain't much with women."

Hackett sensed danger and said, "Ya been in these parts long?"

"Long enough to kill a sheriff."

Hackett leaned forward, watching Draik. "Sheriff, huh? Where at?"

Draik took a lingering drink, licked his lips, and said, "Lodgepole. Fella named Radison, but he ain't the one I really want."

Hackett fingered his glass. "And who might that be?"

"Colter." Draik paused with a distant look, lifted his glass, and continued, "Jed Colter, Deputy U.S. Marshal."

Hackett laughed. "'Fraid you're late, son. Gibbons kilt him a few days back."

Draik's pale eyes lifted up to Hackett. "Ya thought Gibbons killed him. A tie hacker from Cheyenne said Colter was there last night." Draik hesitated, then scoffed, "Oh, he was shot up some, but ya didn't finish the job."

Hackett cursed Gibbons and then himself for not checking on Colter. Suddenly an idea occurred to him.

Hackett drained his glass and belched. "Since you and me want this Colter dead, I'll make ya a deal. Kill Colter and I'll pay ya a hun'erd dollars."

Draik sensed desperation in Hackett. Since he was going to kill Colter anyway, why not get paid for it? A smile played at the corners of his mouth. Draik weighed the offer, drawing hard on the quirly. His eyes met Hackett's and he countered, "Two hundred."

Hackett squirmed, thinking deviously. It was a lot of money, but if he played his cards right he wouldn't have to pay. The thought of facing Colter again chilled Hackett.

"Draik, ya drive a hard bargain. Okay, two hun'erd it is."

A burden lifted as Hackett filled Draik's glass and then his own.

Jim Colter sat on the edge of his bunk, looking around the empty bunkhouse. There was room for ten men, but he had not seen more than five. A fireplace occupied one end while a window on each side provided the only view of the outside. Bunks lined two walls. A table with six chairs was placed in front of the fireplace. Lanterns hung from support posts along with rope and harness.

Little Raven and Johnny Hawk had brought him to John Leach's ranch. A kindly man, Leach took him in without a question, except to ask his name. He ate at Leach's table along with the other hands. Strength was returning to his frail body. Leach had put him to work in the tack room, where he repaired and cared for the cowhand's gear. He had come to like Shorty Gaines, the easygoing bronc buster.

Colter turned a watch over in his hand and thoroughly examined it. He fingered the script letters, *JC*, on the front, and pondered. What did the letters mean? Was it his watch? He opened the cover and observed a woman's picture. She was beautiful, and there was something vaguely familiar in the eyes. Who was she? Colter was baffled as questions peppered his mind.

The memory flashes. Colter's brow wrinkled. What did they mean? There was a family and green carpeted hills and valleys. Tree-shrouded mountains were caped in a blue haze. He looked searchingly at the woman's picture. Was she the wife and mother in his memory flashes?

He put away the watch and reached into a pocket for a soiled and rumpled envelope. The writing had mostly disappeared with time, sweat, rain, and frequent handling. Trembling fingers unfolded the letter. He read it again.

Dearest James,
   The news around here is that the war will end in a matter of months. I hope so. We miss you so much.
   Micah and Ruth are growing so fast. Micah is getting to be quite a handsome young man. The young ladies certainly think so. He has taken over all the manly chores. Ruth is developing fast—too fast. All the young men are taking notice.
   Received a letter from Jed last week. He is still in Sedalia. I do wish he would come home. Maybe after the war is over.

He squinted in the dim light but couldn't make out the remainder of the letter. Scarcely visible at the bottom were the words "Your loving wife, Sarah." Pensively, he folded the letter and put it away. Colter paced the floor and mulled over his thoughts. The names were not familiar. He called himself Sam because he couldn't remember his own name. Who were these people?

The sound of hoofbeats signaled the approach of Leach's cowhands. The chilled air prompted Colter to start a fire. The blaze had caught when Shorty Gaines stepped inside the bunkhouse, followed by several others.

Moving to the fireplace, Shorty chattered, "Sam, it's too early in the year to be gettin' this chilly. Boys, it's gonna be a long, hard winter."

John Leach insisted on one rule: no one leaves the ranch alone. The threat of Indian attacks was ever present. Occasionally, the carcass of a butchered steer was found. Leach figured it was worth a few cattle so long as the Indians left them alone.

Heads turned at the sound of the cowbell.

Venson, the ramrod, said, "Time for grub, boys."

Shorty jested, "We better get there before Sam does. The way he's been eatin', there won't be any left for us."

They moved briskly up the hill to the main house. Colter was happy. He was working and eating well and had a roof over his head, but something was missing. Who was he?

Harley Banes liked his idea. Colter would be looking for him in Cheyenne. He had to leave for Lodgepole before Colter got to Cheyenne; otherwise, there could be trouble. Banes fidgeted and paced alongside the Last Chance Saloon while he waited for Duggan's return with a fresh mount. Banes heard approaching hoofbeats and spun around. It was Duggan, the swarthy, shifty-eyed hardcase who did odd jobs as long as they didn't involve too much work. Duggan's face seemingly had a perpetual sneer. He swung down from the saddle and caught the gold coin Banes tossed him.

Banes took the reins, looked at Duggan, and warned, "Remember, you ain't seen me. If I hear otherwise, I'll kill ya."

Duggan said derisively, "Nobody'll know. 'Specially the law."

Banes crawled into the saddle, skirted around the edge of town, and headed for Lodgepole. Of those who knew him, only Duggan had seen him in Cheyenne. The Westerner's Saloon was on the edge of Lodgepole. He figured that would give him ample opportunity to slip in unnoticed.

Thoughts meandered through his mind. Banes remembered Arneaux and the Indians, then checked his gun and the Winchester. He would get a room over the Westerner's and wait for Colter. A fair fight with Colter was out of the question. It would be from ambush, at close range. Draik had killed the sheriff, so Colter was his only concern. Banes shook his head and chuckled.

"Marshal, you won't know I'm anywhere near."

Banes liked his plan and thought of the beautiful Ellen Wellsley. He could settle down with a woman like her. She would never know who had killed Colter.

He mused, "I'm not a bad-lookin' fella, and I've got enough money to start a respectable life. That bank needs a banker. I could do that."

Banes checked his back trail and warily approached ridges and small rises. He scanned the horizon and glanced up each wash and draw. His plan was set. He didn't need any surprises. The thought of a future with Ellen Wellsley brought a smile.

Ellen sat up, startled. She had heard something. Was she dreaming? Burke had left for Vick's to check on a package he was expecting. Maybe he was back.

"Doc?"

She got no response. Ellen opened the door, but no one was there. Thinking it was a dream, she checked on Radison. Burke did say if Radison made it another twenty-four hours, he would have a chance. She glanced at the clock on the mantle. The twenty-four hours had passed two hours ago. She checked for a fever and found none. Her spirits soared when she found a faint pulse. Ellen turned to get fresh water and a clean cloth when she heard it again.

She spun around. "Luke?"

The groan was barely audible. She took his hand in hers. "Luke, it's Ellen. Can you hear me?"

The slight movement of Radison's hand brought tears cascading down her face.

"Luke, you're going to make it."

Pent-up emotions swept over Ellen like an ocean wave. She rested her head on the table by Radison and wept. Jedidiah had left Lodgepole days ago, and she had not heard a word. He seldom left her thoughts. She had slept little and eaten sparingly since Radison was gunned down.

"Miss Ellen, what's happened?"

Burke gently pulled her away from the table.

Ellen looked up at Burke and took his hand. "Oh Doc, Luke's going to make it. I heard him groan, and I saw his hand move."

Burke patted her hand. "You scared me, Miss Ellen. For a moment, I thought we had lost him."

Burke moved the stethoscope over Radison's chest, listening attentively. He nodded with a faint smile.

"Heartbeat is a bit stronger. He's got a chance to make it, but we must keep him still. If he thrashes around, bleeding could start again."

Ellen wiped away the tears and looked admiringly at Burke.

"Doc, you're the best doctor I've ever known."

"Miss Ellen, your words are too kind. Without you, Luke wouldn't have made it this far." Looking over his glasses, he continued, "You need rest. Go get something to eat, and then go to bed. That's doctor's orders."

Burke placed his hands on her shoulders. With a fatherly look, he said, "It's none of my business, but Marshal Colter will be back."

Ellen put a hand over her tremulous lips, fighting back tears.

Burke smiled and asked, "Did you know that you talk in your sleep?"

She gasped and blushed. "Oh, no!"

Burke chuckled. "Don't worry. That's strictly between doctor and nurse."

Burke and Ellen laughed, relieving the tension enshrouding them.

Jed Colter awoke at dawn, thinking about Banes. Where was he? Colter and Ilsen had searched every corner of Cheyenne. Weems had not seen him. Maybe the Arapaho got him.

Colter lit the lamp and thought of Ellen as he shaved off two days of stubble. She had been on his mind a lot. His anger grew when he thought about what Draik had done to Radison.

Colter buckled his gunbelt and tied down the holster. Where was his father? Frustration was now an enemy. Where should he start looking? O'Quinn and some of Dodge's men were out searching. If his father was in that area, they would find him, but would it be too late? The knot returned to his belly at the thought of Banes, Hackett, and Gibbons. One thing was certain: he would not rest until he found them.

After a pot of coffee and a half dozen eggs and ham, he was chilled by the brisk walk to the livery. Dark, heavy clouds to the west didn't bode well. His slicker would break the wind.

A light snow was falling when Lodgepole came into view. Early snows usually didn't last, and Colter hoped this one wouldn't be the exception. Snow or not, he had to pick up Hackett's trail. He pulled into the livery as Asa Longley shuffled out of the shadows.

"Jed, am I glad to see you!" Longley said. He spit and continued, "Guess you heard about Sheriff Radison?"

Colter eased out of the saddle. "How is he, Asa?"

"Doc thinks Luke's gonna make it. It was turrible. That ugly snake fella shot him three times. I saw it all. Somethin' happ'ned to Luke's gun. He couldn't git it out of the holster. When he did, it was too late."

"He's over at Doc's?" Colter asked, grabbing his saddlebags.

"Yep. Miss Ellen's been with him jist about the whole time." Longley paused, looked at Colter, and added, "She's some lady, Jed."

It didn't surprise Colter. She had the qualities of his mother, and that pleased him.

"Give Smoke a rubdown and grain him good. We're going back out in the morning." Colter thought about Banes. "Any strangers in town?"

Longley rubbed his chin and shook his head. "Nope. Fella from the Westerner's brung over a horse, but I'd seen him before." Longley squinted at Colter and asked, "You have a run-in with somebody?"

Colter threw the saddlebags over his shoulder. "Somebody bushwhacked me over on Lodgepole Creek. Asa, I'll see you in the morning."

Colter's long stride soon brought him to Doc Burke's office. He stepped through the door, escaping the north wind.

Burke got up sluggishly from a chair. "Marshal, welcome back. We've been worried about you."

"Thanks, Doc. How's Luke?"

Burke removed his glasses. "What you're looking at is a miracle," he said thoughtfully.

"Then he's going to make it?" Colter asked hopefully.

"I think so, Jed, but he's got a ways to go. He's not out

of the woods. Miss Ellen and I have been with him the whole time. We can't allow him to move for fear of setting off internal bleeding from that chest wound. Heartbeat is stronger. He's lost a lot of blood. I don't understand why he's alive, but Luke's a fighter. He regained consciousness briefly this morning. This will go on a while longer." Burke hesitated, looking at Colter. "Miss Ellen has been a warrior. I've never seen anyone give as much as that young lady."

Colter nodded. "She's got spirit and grit. I'm going out in the morning, but I can sit with Luke later today if that will help."

Burke smiled wearily. "That would be a big help. It would give Miss Ellen and me a chance to rest some before tonight."

Colter turned to go. "I'll get cleaned up and grab something to eat."

Burke stared at Colter. "Hold on, Jed. What's that around your head?"

"Got ambushed over on Lodgepole Creek."

Burke waved to a chair and said firmly, "Here, sit down and let me take a look at that."

Colter reluctantly removed his hat and sat down. Burke meticulously removed the blood-soaked bandanna from Colter's head. He whistled. "You must be some tough gent to be walking around with this. Does it hurt?"

"Some, but I've been too busy to give it much thought."

Doc stepped back. "I'm going to clean this up and dress it. You shouldn't be doing anything for at least two days."

Colter glanced laconically at Burke. "Doc, I'm leaving in the morning for the Black Hills."

"No, you're not, and that's final." Burke said tersely, and then stopped. "What's this bump on the back of your head?"

Colter argued, "Doc, I'm leaving. I've got no other choice, *and that's final.*"

"Don't be so pigheaded!" Burke gazed over his glasses. "I asked you, what's this bump?"

"Somebody hit me with a shovel."

Burke shook his head. "From the looks of things, you've had some bad days and a lot of headaches."

"Guess you could say that, Doc." Colter winced when Burke touched a tender spot. "I'm still leaving in the morning."

Burke said testily, "When I turn Miss Ellen loose on you, you'll change your mind."

Colter had not seen Burke this firm with anyone. Doc was right. He felt trapped and useless. The trail was getting cold. His father was out there somewhere. Then there was Draik, Banes, Hackett, and Gibbons. Burke was asking a lot. Colter didn't want Ellen fussing over him, although it would be nice to see more of her.

Burke finished cleaning and dressing Colter's wound.

"Thanks, Doc."

Burke scrubbed his hands in a pan of water. He paused and turned his head to face Colter. "Are you going to do like I told you?"

Colter knew he had lost the argument. "Okay, Doc, but it won't be easy."

Drying his hands, Burke said, "Don't figure it to be. You'll thank me when you get up in those hills."

Ellen watched as Colter angled his way to the boarding house. Her heart thumped, and giddiness brought a flush to her cheeks. Why did she feel this way for a man she barely knew?

"Mother, the bath water! Jedidiah's here!"

"Coming right up." Ma giggled, caught up her dress, and stepped briskly up the stairs. Ellen shook her head and smiled.

Colter stood in the door and removed his hat. Ellen paled and stiffled a gasp. "Jedidiah, what happened?"

Colter wanted to bring her to him. He noticed her relief and then her concern when she saw the bandage. Should he tell Ellen how he felt? How would she respond? For now, he would play it safe.

"Tell you later."

"Mother's getting the water ready. Have a seat and I'll get some coffee."

Ellen cocked her head to one side and smiled. Colter's heart pounded. She seemed to get more beautiful each time he saw her.

Ellen poured coffee and continued, "Any word of your father?"

Colter told her what he knew. With two days to kill, he would tell her everything.

Chapter Thirteen

Jed Colter paced like a mountain lion, eager to pick up Hackett's trail. Radison's improvement was encouraging. Colter had found a thread loop near the bottom of Radison's holster and guessed the gunsight had caught the loop, slowing the sheriff's draw.

When he finished eating, he grabbed his hat and started for the door.

"Jed, be careful."

Colter turned to see Ellen by the stairway. Her misty eyes held his for a moment. Suddenly, he didn't want to leave. Colter swallowed hard and fought the urge to take her in his arms, but he scarcely knew her.

After pausing, he said, "I will."

Ellen watched Colter until he got to Doc Burke's office. She caught up her dress and went upstairs, fighting back tears. In her room, she fell across the bed as sobs racked her body. She was mystified. Was she in love with Jed Colter, a man she had known for such a brief time? How did he feel about her?

* * *

Colter checked on Radison and then went to the livery. Crispy air put a spring in his step and seemingly cleared his head.

"Jed, thought you wuz leavin' two days ago."

Asa Longley moved with a noticeable limp—the legacy of many bronc busters.

"Doc is a pretty convincing fella, Asa. He said I'd do well to wait two days before going out."

"Somethin's comin'." Longley leaned on a pitchfork and patted his right leg. "This leg o' mine has acted up the past few days. Never seen it like this. Leastwise, not this early in the year. Don't git caught in a storm up in them hills. It's dangerous up there."

"Thanks, Asa. I think that leg of yours has more sense than the two of us."

Colter saddled Smoke and sensed his readiness to run. He swung into the saddle and smiled as Smoke pranced sideways out of the livery. The grulla had his way and then settled down.

Colter pointed Smoke over the southern rim of the valley. Cresting the rim, he leaned into the wind and turned up the collar of his sheepskin-lined coat. Smoke picked his way through piebald aspen. The scent of pine and juniper permeated the air as Colter passed large boulders and rode over rock-strewn trails.

The Black Hills loomed ahead, silhouetted against the early morning sky. As Colter ascended the hills, his anticipation grew. He didn't expect to find his father with Hackett and Gibbons, but they *would* tell him what happened. Colter was vigilant since Longley had told him of an Arapaho sacred burial ground in the Black Hills.

Smoke patiently picked his way up steep rocky slopes,

crossed meadows, and dropped down into ravines and washes. It took a rugged horse to get around in this country. The grulla was making it look easy. Pronghorn and mule deer scampered away at their approach. Smoke snorted and whinnied at what Colter thought was a distant mountain lion. The alluring beauty of the Black Hills mesmerized Colter. Strange rock formations and mammoth boulders seemingly teetered on almost nothing, waiting patiently for the wind to set them in motion.

It was noon when he emerged from the craggy trail and approached the crest of the Black Hills. Colter eased up and slipped from the saddle to let Smoke blow and nibble on clumps of grass. Beef jerky and Ma's biscuits dimmed his hunger.

After eating, he pulled into the saddle and nudged Smoke toward the western slope. The high meadow wind was fierce and unrelenting. Aspen, like golden spires, glittered in the sun. The surrounding hills were covered, almost black, with lodgepole pine. Colter sensed this was hallowed ground as his gaze swung around the huge meadow. The terrain swelled and dipped like sea waves. He understood why the Indians defended their right to this land.

Colter crested the hills and pulled up sharply. To the west lay a mountain of dark, rolling clouds. Stretching the length of the snowcapped mountains, the portentous beauty of the ominous clouds belied their deadly approach.

"Asa was right. Something is in the making."

Colter's first thought was to get as far down the slope as possible before the storm hit. He angled Smoke down the slope, keeping an eye on the coming storm. He searched for shelter, but none was immediately available. Sensing the impending danger, the grulla rebelled at Colter's commands.

Colter kept a firm hand on the reins while steadily moving Smoke ahead. A broken leg on this treacherous ground and he would be stranded.

The storm was minutes away. Colter spotted a large boulder surrounded by pines to his left. They scrambled to the boulder as the storm unleashed a fury of swirling snow amid a wind that Colter thought would blow them over. Smoke was spooked as wind whistled and howled through the pines. Colter dismounted, took a rope from the saddle, looped it over the grulla's head, and secured it to the nearest tree. Colter shrugged into his slicker, then unfurled his bedroll and draped it over Smoke.

In his haste to get down the slope, Colter failed to make mental notes of landmarks or the horizon. He was lost and couldn't make any sense of it until the storm abated. Colter took the Henry and huddled against the lee side of the boulder. After tugging his hat down low, he gathered the slicker around him to wait out the storm.

Hearing footsteps, John Leach looked up from the papers on his desk. Leach, a widower, finger-combed his thick gray hair that offered a stark contrast with his bronzed, weathered face. Loneliness sometimes clouded his clear blue eyes, but he was quick to smile. The soft Texas drawl belied his rugged features. Like others in these parts, he had come north in search of better grazing land.

"Come in, Sam," Leach said.

To Leach, Sam was an enigma. Why would this man wander afoot on the plains? The Pawnee soldiers had rescued him from the Arapaho. Leach had turned it over in his mind many times and it still didn't add up. Sam was not from these parts. Where had he come from? The railroad? He was in need of clothes and shoes, but he wouldn't take what

Leach had offered. It was obvious Sam was a man of pride and dignity. The way he talked, the straight, even teeth, and the manner in which he carried himself—he was no ordinary drifter. What had happened in Sam's life to put him in this situation? Leach liked the way Sam looked him straight in the eye and the pride he took in his work.

Sam removed his hat. "Mr. Leach, I've come to tell you, I'm leaving with Shorty to go to Lodgepole. I want to thank you for taking me in. Maybe someday I can return the favor."

Leach leaned back in his chair. "Sam, you already have."

Sam's leaving didn't surprise Leach. He would have to find what he had lost.

Leach continued, "You can stay here for as long as you want. The men like you; I like you. You're the best I've ever seen at fixing gear. I'll pay what's coming to you."

Sam nodded. "Thank you, Mr. Leach. I've got some things to attend to in Lodgepole."

Leach reached into a desk drawer and took out a metal box. He counted out the wages, wondering what business Sam had in Lodgepole. Maybe Sam didn't like imposing on his hospitality. Leach debated asking, but he was a curious and direct man.

"Sam," Leach said, then paused, rubbing his chin with a large calloused hand. "Is that your name? I've got this hunch there's something here I don't know about. I'd like to help, but I don't want to pry either. I guess what sticks in my mind is where are you from, and what are you doing out here?"

Sam shifted his feet, stared at the floor, and nervously twisted his hat. His mind raced to think of an answer. "It's Sam Young, Mr. Leach. I'm from West Virginia. I've worked a lot of places. Shorty tells me there's a railroad being laid in these parts. Thought I'd go there to see if they can use me."

Leach was not convinced, and Sam was frustrated. The

man wasn't sure who he was or where he came from. What would become of him? How would he provide for himself? The frontier was an unforgiving place for a defenseless man like Sam. Or was he? Sam said he had killed an Arapaho. He was not a bragging man, but the Pawnees said Sam had killed the Arapaho without a weapon.

Leach pushed back the big highback chair, stood up, and extended his hand. "Sam, you're welcome back here anytime. If I can help you in any way, let me know."

Sam nodded. "Thank you, Mr. Leach."

"When you get to Lodgepole, look up Jed Colter. He's a Deputy U.S. Marshal there. He might be able to help you."

Sam lifted his head, staring intently at Leach. Their eyes held, then Sam said, "You say Colter?"

"That's right. Jed Colter. Know him?"

Sam shook his head, then turned slowly, immersed in thought, and left. Leach followed him out to the porch. He had caught Sam's reaction at the mention of Colter. Was he wanted by the law? Leach pondered then dismissed the thought. He recalled meeting Jed Colter in Lodgepole. Something about Sam reminded him of the marshal.

Shorty Gaines crawled into the seat by one of the other cowhands and flicked the reins. He had brought an extra Winchester for Sam in case they spotted game or ran across Indians. Sam was distant, like something was on his mind.

The flashes of memory haunting Sam were becoming more frequent. He could make no sense of them. In the last memory, he was with a Colonel John Mosby, planning an attack on an encampment of soldiers. Mosby had called them Union forces. Sam remembered wearing a gray uniform, and Mosby had called him Colter. Or was it somebody else he had called Colter?

Gaines said, "There's Lodgepole. Sam, we'll stop by the livery. I want you to meet Asa Longley. He runs the place and might have somethin' for you to do."

Gaines pulled the wagon up at the livery entrance as Longley limped out of the shadows.

"Howdy, Asa. Got somebody I want you to meet." Gaines nodded in Sam's direction and continued. "This here's Sam, the best tackman I ever saw. Thought maybe you could use some help."

Longley shielded his eyes from the sun. "Boy, ya still bustin' broncs?"

Gaines nodded. "Yep."

Longley spit and wiped a sleeve across his mouth. "Take some advice and git outta the business or you'll wind up like me." He squinted an eye over at Sam. "Sam, is it? Jist so happens I got more'n I can do here at the moment. Light down, and we'll git started. Pay ain't much, though."

Sam said, "Thank you, Mr. Longley. Pay's not that important."

Gaines smiled and extended a hand. "Sam, you know where to find us."

"Thanks for everything, Shorty. I'll keep that in mind."

Sam eased off the wagon and joined Longley. Gaines watched them fade into the shadows of the livery. He shook his head, wondering about Sam.

Meanwhile, two eyes, blurred from too much whiskey and not enough sleep, watched from an upstairs window of the Westerner's Saloon.

"Doc, when am I gittin' outta this bed?"

Burke smiled mischievously. "Sheriff, you can get up now."

Radison gasped and settled back in bed. Weakly, Radison asked, "How much longer, Doc?"

Burke turned in his chair, watching the sheriff.

"If you're a fast healer, maybe another week. You've lost a lot of blood. It'll take time for you to even stand up. I suggest patience, and one other thing. You can thank Miss Ellen."

"Doc, she's somethin', ain't she?" He turned his head toward Burke and continued. "I thank she's took a likin' to Jed. He can't say I didn't warn him."

"Warn him about what?"

"I told the marshal out on the prairie to be careful or that philly would rope and hawgtie him."

Burke smiled, then a solemn look crossed his face. "I'm going to ask you something, 'cause *she's* going to ask you."

Radison asked dubiously, "Ask me what, Doc?"

"That wedding ring on your finger. What's that all about? You have a wife?"

Radison fell silent, fixing his eyes on the ceiling. He clenched his teeth and swallowed.

Burke didn't push, but waited for Radison's reply.

Suddenly, Radison's voice grew haggard. "Doc, I'll tell ya on one condition."

"What's that?"

"I could never tell Miss Ellen." Radison paused, then looked at Burke. "Would ya tell her for me?"

"I'll tell her," Burke assured and pulled up a chair.

Radison closed his eyes, took a deep breath, and grimaced as he expelled it in a ragged fashion. His voice shook.

"Some years back—I weren't no older than twenty, I guess—I had a little spread down on the Brazos and a wife. Rebecca wuz her name. We had a few head of cattle and they wuz just beginnin' to grow. Early one mornin' I left to check a bog that had claimed one of my calves. I wuz gone most of the mornin' just checkin' on one thang and another."

Radison stopped to gather himself. His eyes fluttered open a moment, then closed again. Soon, he continued. "When I got back to the house 'round mid-mornin', there wuz two horses hitched to the porch. Horses I'd never seen. I didn't like the looks of thangs, so I come up on the backside of the house and heard men laughin' and throwin' thangs around inside. I knew Rebecca was in trouble, so I slipped 'round to the porch as they come out the door. I got the drop on 'em, but they went for their irons anyway. I gutshot one and hit the other in the leg. I got their irons, and then took their horses to the corral where they couldn't git to 'em without help from me." Radison paused to catch his breath and went on, "I went inside to see about Rebecca. They'd beat her so bad, Doc, that she died in my arms. She'd told me a month earlier that we wuz goin' to have a baby."

Radison grew silent, and Burke patiently waited. Radison's eyes glistened. Burke understood his agony of recalling that day.

"Doc, somethin' jist went off inside me. I jist went crazy. I went outside and tied the one I shot in the leg to a post, knowin' the other one wuzn't goin' nowhere. The one I gutshot, I put him on his horse and took him to a big oak tree 'bout a hun'erd yards out. He was purty far gone, bein' gutshot 'n all. I put a rope 'round his neck and hung him to finish him off. I wanted the other one to see what wuz goin' to happen to him. When he saw the other one swingin', he started squealin' and tryin' to git away. I took my time—I wanted him to suffer before I sent him to hell. I even had a smoke while I watched him squirm. I untied him from that post, and then tied his hands behind his back. Then I put him on his horse and led him to the tree and let him git a good look at the other one swingin'. I got me another rope and put it 'round his neck and then untied his hands. I've never seen such a coward. He cried for mercy, but Doc, there weren't no mercy in me that day."

Radison hesitated, then continued. "I left them hangin' there and pinned a note on them both sayin' that they'd kilt my wife and unborn child. I buried Rebecca and left that day and never went back. I couldn't. Not without my Rebecca. I ain't proud of what I done, Doc, but I did what I had to do. They wuz Draik's brothers. That's why he come after me."

Radison had talked himself out. Burke knew Radison had just relived every grizzly moment of that day, just as he often did the day his Mollie died. In a way, he wished he had not asked about the ring.

Burke pushed back his chair and stood. "Luke, I'm sorry I put you through that. I'll tell Miss Ellen. Now try to get some rest."

Burke turned as the door opened. Ellen smiled, setting the basket of food on his desk. Seeing the look on Burke's face, she asked, "Doc, is something wrong?"

Burke, feeling the sting of Radison's story, shook his head. As Ellen drew closer, he whispered, "Luke told me about his wife."

As Burke recounted what Radison had told him, Ellen saw the sadness in his eyes. Burke removed his glasses and slumped in a chair.

The solemnity of the moment was broken as five cavalrymen rode past Burke's office.

"Wonder what the cavalry's doing here," Burke mused as they watched the soldiers pull up and dismount at Ma's.

"I better go see what's going on," Ellen said, leaving Burke's office.

She watched the soldiers as they grouped by their mounts and talked among themselves. As she approached, an officer stepped away from the group and removed his hat.

"Ma'am, I'm Captain Bert Kilbane from Fort Russell. I'm looking for Marshal Jed Colter."

Ellen froze, clenching her fists. The years and many battles had matured him since that day when young Lieutenant Kilbane brought her the news of Easton's death. She stood silent as the years rolled back, renewing the anguish, the solitude.

Chapter Fourteen

Jed Colter awoke with a start. He got up and flexed his arms and legs. Smoke stood lazy, head down. The snow had lessened to a steady downfall of smaller flakes. Footing would be treacherous, but he had no other choice than to lead Smoke down the slope.

"Smoke, we've got to get down this slope before dark."

The grulla whinnied softly when Colter offered a sugar lump. Colter looped the reins over the pommel and took the lead rope. Gripping the Henry in his left hand, he moved deliberately, searching for the best path. Wind whistled up the slope and swept snow into drifts.

An hour had passed since Colter began to pick his way down the slope. His body ached with each tedious step. Boulders and serrated rock dappled the terrain. Colter searched for a wall or overhang where he could make camp.

The bandanna over his head did little to keep the wind off his ears. Wind swirled and picked up intensity, bringing another maelstrom of snowflakes. Realizing he was lost, Colter kept moving. Longley's warning had become a reality. When the ground leveled out, Colter stopped to get his bearings, but all he saw was an alabaster wall of snow. The grulla tossed his head, ears pricked forward.

"What is it, Smoke?" Colter asked softly.

Colter removed the bandanna, held his breath, and listened. Smoke whinnied, this time louder. Colter cocked his ear and heard the faint protest of a burro or mule. He figured it came from his left, and he groped his way in that direction.

If Hackett and Gibbons were nearby, he had the element of surprise on his side. Slowly, Colter moved forward, then paused when he saw a flickering light through the trees. He eased forward and then stopped. A solitary figure hunched over the fire.

"Hello there!" Colter yelled.

A man lurched clumsily to his feet, befuddled by the intrusion. Colter entered the circle of light, facing the slight frame of an old man.

The stranger gathered himself and said, "Mister, ya jist about skeer'd my britches off. What'cha doin' way out here anyhow?"

"Name's Jed Colter, Deputy U.S. Marshal out of Lodgepole."

"Pike, Wiley Pike. Been doin' some prospectin' and trappin' in these parts, but I ain't had much luck." Pike gestured and said, "Come up to the fire, boy, and let me git a look at'cha."

Pike leaned forward and squinted. "Did ya say Colter?"

"That's right, Jed Colter."

Pike's eyes widened, then he asked, "Would ya be kin o' John Colter that roamed these parts?"

Colter nodded. "My grandfather's brother."

"Boy, he wuz a heap o' man. Met him once when I wuz

jist a pup. Ya got his eyes, boy, and from what I recollect, ya got his looks."

Mostly by choice, these men led lonely lives. Pike was older than most men he had seen in these parts. A floppy hat pushed back on his head revealed a shock of white hair. A tendril hung down over his brow. Tobacco-stained, frosty whiskers caught snowflakes. Fringed buckskin hung on a thin body too frail for a rugged environment. Colter wondered how men like Pike survived in these elements.

Colter secured Smoke to a nearby tree, then hunkered by the fire and warmed his hands. Pike had picked an overhang to wait out the storm. A line of spruce and aspen buffered the wind. Pike chewed the quid, shifting it from cheek to cheek.

"Mr. Pike, I'm looking for a couple of men, name of Hackett and Gibbons. They have a wagon fitted like a jail and three prisoners with them."

Pike knelt by the fire and shot a stream of juice hissing into the flames.

"I see'd one o' them fellas. A big redheaded gent with a badge. He had a wagon like ya said and three pris'ners. Didn't say what his name was. Wouldn't let me nigh any o' them pris'ners. Peculiar actin' fella. Said he wuz takin' them pris'ners to Cheyenne and had got lost." Pike chuckled and added, "He's a fer distance from Cheyenne."

Looking at Pike across the fire, Colter's hopes surged. "Where did they go from here?"

"I told him 'bout an old mine jist down the crick 'bout a mile or so." Pike nodded the direction. "Said he'd hole up there 'til this weather clears."

Pike reached a knobby hand to the ground and brushed away leaves. With a small stick, he drew a crude map in the dirt.

"Now, boy, we're here." Pike indicated with an X, then went on, "Jist follow this here crick 'bout a mile and you'll see this outcroppin' o' rock. Jist to the right o' them rocks is some scrubby pine. Behind them pines is a cave. That's where they'll be."

Colter made a mental note of the map. "Thanks, Mr. Pike. I've got something for you."

Colter brought over the sack with Ma's biscuits and passed it to Pike. The old man sniffed a biscuit. After a bit, his eyes lit up.

"Ain't had one o' these in many a season."

Pike grinned toothlessly, then continued, "Say, boy, what'cha want with this Hackett and Gibbons?"

Colter told him, and after a fill of jerky, biscuits, and coffee, they bedded down for the night. Wind moaned lonely and haunting through the trees and around the overhang. Colter turned his back to the fire and pulled the bedroll up around his ears. Thoughts of Ellen allayed a restless night.

Colter awakened to the stirring of Pike and fresh-brewed coffee. Through the night they had kept the fire burning. Colter put away his bedroll and retrieved the string of animal teeth he had taken from the body of the old Indian in Mesa Canyon.

"Mr. Pike, you ever see anything like this?"

Pike held the string near the fire, squinting in the dim light. He fingered individual teeth and examined the markings.

"Boy, I see'd somethin' like this when I spent a week with the Blackfoot. Where'd ya git it?"

Colter told Pike about his encounter with the Indian.

"I hear'd tell that one of them young bucks that wuz after ya uncle John never did give up the chase and never returned to his tribe." Pike spit in the fire and added, "Don't know if that's true or not. I figger when that old Injun saw ya, he thought he wuz a lookin' at the ghost of John Colter."

Colter prepared to break camp, then cinched up the saddle and pulled atop the grulla.

"Mr. Pike, I would feel better if you would come back to Lodgepole with me. This is no place for any man."

Pike looked out across the rugged mountains and with a sweep of an outstretched arm said "This is where I belong, boy."

A light snow fell as Colter followed the creek. From the look of things the snow would soon stop. He rounded a sharp bend of the creek and abruptly pulled up when he saw the outcropping of rock. Pike had drawn a good map.

Colter scanned the surroundings, but didn't see any movement. He nudged Smoke forward until he neared the rock. Several levels of rock stairstepped up and then leveled off. Colter swung from the saddle, rousing a snowshoe rabbit that scurried through the snow and disappeared behind a rock. A pronghorn watched curiously from a distance, then nonchalantly pawed at a clump of grass. He snubbed Smoke to a scrub oak, then checked his gun and sheathed it. Pulling the Henry, Colter began the climb up the rock.

Colter scrambled to the top and then paused to catch his breath. He drew the Colt and eased forward, keeping close to the craggy rock wall extending majestically above him. Colter stopped where the wall curved to the left. Peeking around the wall, he saw the patch of scrubby pine and the wagon.

He whispered, "You were right, old-timer. Gibbons *is* here!"

Colter worked his way forward, hugging the wall. He paused, listening for any sound, and scanned every rock and crevice. Colter stepped around a jagged, slanted piece of rock and suddenly stopped. The mine entrance was only a few feet away. He drew back behind the rock to gather his thoughts.

Colter took a deep breath and stepped around the rock with his eyes fixed on the mine entrance. His foot slipped on loose shale that made a tinkling sound as it skittered across the rocky surface. He froze, listening. Hearing voices, Colter quickly ducked behind the rock, dropped to a knee, and peeked. Two men emerged from the mine. The one with a rifle, he guessed, was Gibbons. If they came his way, Colter would be forced to make a play. If Gibbons went out too far on the rocky shelf, he would see Smoke.

Gibbons and the rail-thin, shaggy-whiskered man paused to let their eyes adjust to the light. Colter's heart pounded as Gibbons prodded the other man with his rifle. He breathed easier when they rounded a large boulder. Was Hackett in the mine? Colter pondered this as he crossed the distance to the mine entrance where decaying, splintered timbers were crisscrossed like matchsticks. He glanced over his shoulder, then stepped into the shadows. Hearing muffled voices, he moved deeper into the mine. With each tentative step, the voices became more audible. Colter glanced over his shoulder. Fetid air hung like a swamp fog. His boot struck a rock, echoing into the mine. The voices hushed as he moved forward until he saw a light. Colter hugged a wall as he inched forward. He stopped at the sound of scuffling feet behind him.

Realizing he had to chance it, Colter positioned himself to see the lantern and the surrounding mine. Two men, each wrapped in a blanket, sat by the lantern. A mining cart and empty crates were lined along one wall. Behind them, the mine veered off at a right angle. He swiftly covered the distance, startling the men.

Colter put a finger to his lips, then whispered urgently, "I'm Marshal Jed Colter! Is Hackett here?"

Amazement masked their faces before one said, "No, Marshal! Colter?"

Footsteps drew nearer. Colter looked over his shoulder, then cautioned them, "Quiet, Gibbons is coming."

Colter bolted deeper into the mine and faded into the darkness. The two prisoners gaped at each other, speechless.

Gibbons and the prisoner came into the circle of light. Leaning the rifle against a far wall, he eased himself down and rested his back against a timber.

"What's all that noise I heard?" Gibbons growled, and scornfully added, "You two tryin' to cook up somethin'?"

One of the prisoners said, "Could be, Gibbons. I got this feelin' you'll remember this day until they put a rope 'round your neck. I hear there ain't no cure for hemp fever."

The two prisoners laughed as the third looked on, puzzled at their boldness.

Gibbons snapped, "Shut your mouth, Cain, or you'll never leave this mine alive."

An edgy Gibbons stared scornfully at the prisoners. Cain had been outspoken before, but he had never seen him this bold. Gibbons didn't like the tone of Cain's voice and figured something was amiss. His head swiveled while his beady eyes darted around the mine. Then he reached for the rifle.

A voice caromed off the walls. "Hold it, Gibbons!"

Colter leveled the .44 menacingly at Gibbons. The outlaw's jaw gaped while his face blanched like he had seen a ghost. His hand froze inches from the rifle.

Gibbons quavered. "Where'd ya come from?"

Cain laughed. "He's a haint, Gibbons, come to take ya to hell."

"Never mind where I came from." Colter glowered at Gibbons, then motioned with his Colt. "Move away from that rifle."

Gibbons' eyes grew wild and fixed on Colter as he inched to his right.

Colter continued, "I'm Deputy U.S. Marshal Jed Colter. Jim Colter is my father."

Gibbons ran his tongue over dry lips and stammered, "No! Colter, I–I kilt ya back on Lodgepole Crick!"

"Then you're talking to a ghost," Colter said disdainfully. His hostile eyes bore into Gibbons while he motioned with the .44. "Get up, Gibbons, and carefully unbuckle that gunbelt and kick it over here."

Gibbons did as he was told.

Colter glanced at the prisoners. "One of you men get his gunbelt and somebody come around behind me and take his rifle."

Shackles clanked as two men moved about gathering Gibbons' guns. Their unbelieving eyes seldom left Colter.

"Gibbons, where is the key to those shackles?" Colter asked.

"Come and git it," Gibbons sneered.

Colter's eyes blazed fury. "You don't want me to do that." Then he shouted, "Toss it to the prisoners!"

Gibbons hesitated, then reached into a pocket and threw the key at the prisoners. They scrambled about in the dusky light until one of them found the key. One by one the shackles came off. Colter tossed the Henry to the nearest spellbound prisoner, then unbuckled his gunbelt.

"I'm going to give you something you didn't give these men—a fighting chance. If you take me, then you'll have to deal with them. But first, where is my father?"

"We dumped him north o' the tracks. I figger he went crazy. Wouldn't work, wouldn't talk. He wuz no use to us anymore. The Injuns pro'bly got him."

"Where's Hackett?"

"Holed up with a fella by the name o' Draik in one o' them tie hacker camps."

Colter cocked his head. "Draik? He in cahoots with Hackett?"

Gibbons shrugged. "Don't know. None o' my business."

Colter tossed his gunbelt to a prisoner. Watching Gibbons, Colter removed his coat and threw it aside.

Colter said, "Let's see how you handle someone who can fight back."

Gibbons' face flushed with anger. A barroom brawler, Gibbons snarled, then lowered his head and lunged. Colter nimbly sidestepped and stuck out a foot, catching Gibbons' ankle. Gibbons stumbled into a support timber and cursed. He picked himself up, glared at Colter, and rushed in again. Colter planted his feet and feinted to his left. Gibbons took it, and Colter chopped a short left under the heart. He gasped as Colter moved in with a right to the chin. Glassy-eyed, Gibbons fell forward and grabbed Colter's vest. Colter attempted to pull away, but Gibbons hung on and wrapped an arm around his waist. Gibbons growled like a bear as his powerful arms closed like a vise. A clublike blow to Gibbons' kidney had little effect.

"Come on, Marshal, git outta that grip," one of the prisoners exhorted. The others joined him, shouting encouragement.

Feeling the increasing pressure of Gibbons' arms, Colter brought up a knee to the groin. Colter slammed his knee into Gibbons again and felt the vise grip loosen. Jamming his hands under Gibbons' stubbled chin, Colter pushed hard. Gibbons stumbled back in pain. An uppercut straightened Gibbons and a right to the belly dropped his jaw open. A flurry of blows sent Gibbons staggering against the rock wall. Colter closed in on Gibbons, oblivious to the prisoners' shouts. A right crushed Gibbons' nose, bringing a stream of blood and a shout of pain. Colter stepped back as Gibbons slumped to the ground.

One of the prisoners warned, "Marshal, he's got a knife inside his belt in the back."

Colter found the knife and searched for other weapons. He turned to the prisoners to find his rifle leveled at him.

"Hold it right thar. You say you're a marshal. How do we know you're not one of Hackett's friends?"

"What are you doing, Cain?" asked a prisoner.

"I don't trust nobody no more," Cain said.

Another prisoner said, "Raisin', can't you see the marshal is Captain Colter's kin? Look at the eyes. Why, he looks just like the captain."

"Take it easy, Cain," Colter said. He reached into a pocket and brought out a paper, then continued, "I'm Jed Colter, Captain Jim Colter's son. Here is a telegram from my mother telling me of his disappearance from Point Lookout."

A prisoner read the paper, then nodded and passed it to Cain.

The prisoner asked, "Your mother's name?"

"Sarah Colter of Abingdon, Virginia."

"That does it, Cain. He wouldn't know that if he wasn't the Captain's son."

Cain sheepishly lowered the rifle.

"I don't blame you for being skeptical," Colter said, then added, "One of you men put the shackles on Gibbons."

"It'll be our pleasure, Marshal," Cain said, and stepped forward. "I'm Ephraim Cain from West Virginny. Folks call me Raisin'. I rode with Stonewall Jackson."

Colter took the hand Cain offered. Cain's scarred face grinned through the scraggly beard. The gangly frame hunched forward at the shoulders.

"Marshal, I'm Matt Acker from the Rappahannock area." Acker extended a hand from beneath the tattered blanket. "I rode with Captain Colter and Colonel Mosby."

Colter felt Acker's firm grip and saw hope in his eye. A soiled patch covered Acker's left eye. The bushy beard made his head appear unusually large.

"I'm Buck Trendell, Marshal. Rode with Jeb Stuart. My folks live near New Market." Colter gripped Trendell's large hand. Trendell was six feet or better and broad of shoulder. Attempted trimmings of his thick beard had left it uneven.

"Men, call me Jed," Colter said, looking them over. "What can you tell me about my father?"

Colter sat entranced as Cain, Acker, and Trendell took turns telling how Jim Colter had fought for them, encouraged them. They told of the beatings by Hackett. These men, gaunt and hollow-eyed, were not ashamed as tears trickled down their cheeks. They were young in years, but looked much older. Their spirits soared at the realization of freedom.

"Jed, your father said you would find us. He never lost faith. I wish he was here . . ." Acker's voice broke before he could finish.

Cain draped an arm around Acker's shoulders and said, "Matt wuz close to ya pa, since they rode together with Mosby and all."

Colter held up a hand. "Men, if we hope to make Lodgepole by nightfall, we need to get started. What about the wagon team? Are they in shape to pull that wagon?"

Cain said, "Jed, them mules is 'bout skinny as we arc. They wouldn't git far with that wagon." Acker and Trendell nodded agreement.

Colter paused, then made his decision. "Here's what we'll do. Matt, you and Buck take Gibbons down to that creek and get him cleaned up. Raisin', take these blankets and get the mules ready to ride and I'll get what food I've got."

Cain said, "Ya shore got a way jist like the captain."

Acker and Trendell prodded Gibbons down to the creek. Cain gathered the mules and had them ready as Colter pulled up Smoke. Colter looked over the boney mules and wondered of they would make it to Lodgepole. The difficult part would be getting up the slope. Once they crested, then it would be easier. Colter had three biscuits and some beef jerky that he split among them.

Colter said, "Gentlemen, that will have to do until we get to Lodgepole."

Trendell smiled. "Jed, that's the best food I've had since I left home."

"We'll put Gibbons on one of the mules." Colter turned in the saddle and looked at Trendell. "Buck, you and Matt ride the other one, and Raisin', you ride with me."

The snow had ceased and patches of blue sky were showing through the last remnants of the storm clouds. The wind had lessened to a steady breeze. Colter led the way as the sullen Gibbons followed, with Acker and Trendell bringing up the rear.

Chapter Fifteen

Mystified, Bert Kilbane asked, "Ma'am, is something wrong?"

Ellen was retrospective. "Captain Kilbane, I'm Ellen Wellsley. Please forgive me. Seeing you brought back memories."

Kilbane nodded. "My apologies, Miss Wellsley. I remember the day."

Regaining composure, Ellen extended her hand. "Please call me Ellen, Captain."

Kilbane smiled, removed a glove, and took her hand. "Only if you call me Bert."

Ellen turned her eyes up at Kilbane. "You and your men come over to the boarding house for coffee, and food if you're hungry."

"Thank you. We don't have much time. You know where Jed might be?"

Ellen fell in alongside Kilbane and replied, "He left early yesterday to search for two men up in the Black Hills. They're holding prisoners who were smuggled out of a

Union prison camp. He suspects they're using them as labor on the railroad. His father was among the prisoners at one time. We don't know where he is or if he's alive."

Kilbane and his men followed Ellen into Ma's.

"Mother, this is Captain Bert Kilbane and his men from Fort Russell." After Ma's lack of discernment, Ellen added, "Remember? He brought the news of David's death."

"Oh yes!" Ma said. "It's good to see you again."

"Ma'am, it's my pleasure."

Ma motioned and said, "You men sit and I'll get some coffee."

Kilbane removed his hat. "Ellen, tell me more about Jed and his father."

Ellen recounted what she knew while Kilbane listened intently. The way she said Colter's name and her concerned look told him there was something special between Ellen and his friend.

Kilbane paused, taking a swallow of coffee. "We heard about Sheriff Radison and knew Jed was on the move. I'll leave two of my men here until Jed gets back."

Ellen smiled. "He would like that."

Kilbane pushed back his chair and stood. "How is Sheriff Radison?"

"He's going to make it, but it'll be a long recovery."

"I hope to see you and Jed soon. We have dances occasionally at Fort Russell. Maybe you two could come over."

Ostensibly preoccupied, Ellen smiled. "I would like that very much. I think Jed would too. He will be so happy to see you again."

Kilbane left Ellen with rampant, oppressive memories of David Easton. Sadness etched her face and gloom clouded her eyes.

Ellen said, "Mother, I'm going out for a while."

Ma watched Ellen leave and understood her torment. Then she thought about Jed Colter and smiled, hoping he was all right.

Ellen's walk meandered aimlessly. Her thoughts were conflicted; first Easton, then Colter. Suddenly, tentacles of fear clutched her when she saw dark clouds rolling over the Black Hills.

"Miss Ellen."

Ellen looked up and saw Asa Longley at the livery entrance and movement in the shadows.

"Mr. Asa, how are you?"

Longley chuckled, "Oh, I'm doin' much better since Sam come along."

"Sam?"

"Yes, ma'am." Longley nodded, smiling like a kid with a prize. "Sam, he come in with one of John Leach's men. Mighty handy with the tack work." Longley turned and shouted, "Sam, come out here! I want ya to meet Miss Ellen."

A moment passed while Sam worked his way through the horses and piles of hay.

Longley said, "Sam, this here's Miss Ellen. She's Ma's daughter and she's helpin' Doc Burke with the doctorin' on Sheriff Radison."

Ellen smiled. "Hello, Sam."

Sam removed his hat, revealing a crop of salt-and-pepper hair. After a shy glance, Sam's gaze met Ellen's. His piercing blue eyes mesmerized her. Had she seen those eyes before? Jed! He had those same eyes . . . and the hair! Ellen held her breath. Was Sam Jed's father?

Ellen threw restraint aside. "Mr. Colter?"

Befuddled, Sam looked at Longley and then at Ellen. Frustration blanketed his face, then he mumbled, "No. I'm Sam."

He touched his hat brim and walked into the shadows. Ellen's eyes followed him. The voice! Longley looked at Ellen, confused.

"Miss Ellen, what are ya talkin' 'bout? That's not Mr. Colter, that's Sam."

Ellen leaned over and whispered, "Asa, have you noticed Sam's eyes? Jed has those same eyes and that voice!"

Longley fidgeted, shuffled his feet, and then looked over his shoulder toward Sam.

Bewildered, he asked, "Are ya sayin' Sam here is Jed's pa?"

"I'm not sure." She touched Longley's arm and continued. "Don't say anything until Jed gets back, and don't let Sam out of your sight."

"Yes, ma'am."

Pug Hackett stuck his head through the tent flap and felt the north wind's bite. It had stopped snowing, and sunbeams pierced through the pines. Not seeing Gibbons or the prisoners, he cursed and turned toward the bar. Hackett's toe caught the leg of a chair, knocking it over. He cursed again, grabbed the chair, and threw it across the tent, where it landed on a table and ricocheted into the tent wall.

Draik silently played solitaire, amused by Hackett's edginess.

"C'mon, Hackett, how 'bout a game?" Draik challenged. "Ya gotta give me a chance to win back some of my money."

"Pug!" The hysterical voice called out.

Hackett turned as a runt of a man burst through the tent flap and blurted out, "Pug, one of the hackers saw Gibbons and the prisoners down a ways! They was free and Gibbons was in shackles and there was another big fella, maybe a lawman!"

The little man spoke with a thick Irish brogue. Hackett

grabbed a handful of the Irishman's coat and snarled, "Man, speak English. What are ya sayin'?"

"He's sayin' Colter done caught up with Gibbons," Draik said coolly.

Hackett wheeled around and glared. Draik lazily lifted his gaze up to Hackett. A quirly drooped from his lips and his right eye was slitted to avoid the upward curl of smoke.

Wild-eyed, Hackett said, "Ya gonna sit there all day, Draik? When are ya gonna earn that money? Let's go after 'em!"

Draik continued playing solitaire. "Git a hold of yoreself, Hackett. They ain't goin' nowhere but Lodgepole. We'll move when I think the time is right."

"I think the time is right now!"

Draik laid the cards on the table and deliberately moved back his chair. He stood, flipping the quirly near two tie hackers. His cold, hard eyes leveled on Hackett.

"Ya want to face Colter alone?" Draik prodded. "If so, ya better git goin', but leave the two hundred. We have a deal, remember?"

Hackett scowled, spun on a heel, and headed for the bar.

The sun nestled amid the serrated snow-laden western peaks when Jed Colter drew up atop the rim of the valley. Raisin' Cain slipped to the ground, and Colter stepped out of the saddle to give the animals a breather.

Colter surveyed the valley below. "That's Lodgepole, men."

Colter smiled, removed his hat, and ran a forearm across his brow. His eyes swept the length of the town. Colter's heart raced at the thought of seeing Ellen again.

Dropping to a knee, Cain said, "That shore is a purty sight, Jed."

Gibbons sulked and sneered while Cain, Acker, and Trendell reveled in their freedom.

Exhausted, Colter crawled into the saddle, followed by Cain. The loquacious Cain had chattered like a jaybird during their ride to Lodgepole. He told where Hackett and Gibbons had taken the prisoners after smuggling them out of Point Lookout. Hackett had worked deals with coal miners in West Virginia and Kentucky as he had with Banes on the railroad. Somehow, Hackett had kept one step ahead of the law.

Purposefully, they moved up Main Street. Judson Vick paused on the boardwalk and silently watched them pass. Longley observed curiously from the livery. Sam's eyes lingered on Gibbons and then the lawman. Burke stepped out his office door.

"Welcome back, Marshal," Burke said, and then asked, "Your father?"

Colter shook his head. "Nothing yet, Doc. How's Radison?"

"Meaner by the day," Burke said and threw up his hands. "I don't know how much longer I can put up with him."

Colter wagged his head and smiled. Ellen stood, framed in the window of Ma's. He returned her wave.

A blue-coated soldier, small of stature, poked his head out the jail door as they approached and dismounted.

"Marshal, I'm Corporal Quigley from Fort Russell." Colter took the hand Quigley proffered. "Captain Kilbane told Private Zeman and me to stay here until you got back."

Colter looked sharply at Quigley. "Bert's here?"

"No, sir. He returned to Fort Russell yesterday."

"Will he be back?"

"I'm sure he will, sir."

Colter gestured toward Gibbons. "Corporal, I have a prisoner, Abe Gibbons. In the morning go back to Fort Russell and find out if Sergeant Abe Gibbons is wanted for desertion." Colter lifted his chin toward Cain, Acker, and Trendell.

"These men tell me Gibbons was in charge of the prison guards at Point Lookout. He disappeared the same time these men were smuggled out of Point Lookout in March of '65."

"Yes, sir."

Colter turned to enter the jail. "One other thing, Corporal. Telegrams should be sent to the families of these men. I'll get the information to you in the morning."

"Yes, sir."

Colter pushed Gibbons into the jail and led him to a cell. Gibbons looked away from Colter's frosty glare.

"Don't git too comfortable, Gibbons. You won't be there long." Cain chuckled, then put a hand around his neck and made a choking sound.

Colter turned on a heel and headed for the door. "Men, let's go to Ma's."

Ellen met them at the door. "Jed, thank God you're back! It looked to be a terrible storm up in the hills." Her eyes held Colter's for a moment and then shifted to the other men.

Colter said, "Men, I want you to meet Miss Ellen Wellsley. Ellen, these men were taken prisoner along with my father."

After introductions, Ellen said, "Gentlemen, I am so happy for you. Come in, you all must be very hungry."

Cain said, "Ma'am, we been hungry since '65."

Colter drew back and said, "I'll take Smoke and the mules to the livery and join you later."

"Jed."

The soft voice stopped Colter in his tracks.

Ellen debated telling him. What if Sam was not his father? Wouldn't it be better if he met Sam before anything was said?

Ellen's hypnotic gaze held Colter's. "I'll tell you later. I better help Mother take care of the men." Colter lingered, thinking it odd she had not asked about his father.

Colter made it to the livery with Smoke and the mules in

tow. Twilight was fading to darkness when Longley came out to meet him.

Asa smiled. "Jed, did ya git one of them fellas ya wuz after?"

Colter nodded. "Fella named Gibbons."

"Never see'd him before. Smoke, ya look tired, old son," Longley opined and glanced at the mules. "Them mules don't look like they been fed in a month."

Colter loosened the cinches and caught movement, then he heard the rustle of hay. "Asa, you got somebody back there with you?"

"Oh, yeah. That's Sam. Drifted in here yesterday with one of John Leach's men. Good with horses and gear, so I put him to work. He's cleaned up and done some thangs I meant to do last year. Don't talk much, though. Guess we'll git used to one another."

Longley leaned forward, staring at Colter.

Jed looked up and met Longley's stare. "Something wrong, Asa?"

"Oh, no." Longley shook his head. "Jist glad you're back."

Longley sent a stream of tobacco juice into the livery dust. He suppressed a call for Sam, thinking he had better wait like Miss Ellen said. She would know how to handle it.

Colter left Longley, wondering what had gotten into him. Asa acted peculiar. Come to think of it, so did Ellen. A frown creased his forehead as he turned over these thoughts. Something was up. He could feel it.

Sam watched the marshal leave. Longley had called him Jed. Had not John Leach told him about a Marshal Jed Colter in Lodgepole? Didn't Miss Ellen call him Jed? Earlier, Sam saw him bring in a big redhead. He had seen that one before! The other men! He had seen them too! The memory flashes! Sam paced the livery. The picture was coming into focus, like having a name on the tip of the tongue but not remembering.

Longley called out, "Sam, wanna help me with these mules?"

It rankled Sam that he was so close but couldn't remember. He silently took the mules. Longley's eyes followed him. Sam was distant and Longley wondered what was bothering him.

Harley Banes heard voices and hoofbeats. He rushed to the window of his room over the Westerner's Saloon. With a finger, he parted the curtain. *Colter! He had Gibbons and the prisoners!* Banes cursed. *Where is Hackett? Did Colter get him too?* His palms moistened. The time was near when Colter would pay for what he had done to Harley Banes. A tentative smile played on his lips. Banes closed the curtain as Colter looked up. *Did the marshal see him? Did Colter know he was here?* Doubt gnawed at his belly like a starved coyote. Banes mulled this over and glanced in the mirror on the far wall. His gaze swung around the drab room. The lumpy bed, a table, and washstand served the purpose for which the room was used. Banes clenched his fists. He could do better than this, and he would. Taking a bottle from the table, he filled the glass. In a stupor, he watched the amber rise until it spilled over the rim. A tremor was evident as he lifted the glass to his lips.

"Harley, ain't ya gonna pour Annie a drink?" the squeaky voice asked.

Banes turned to the girl, lost in thought. Annie's job was to mingle with the customers downstairs and separate them from their money. She fluttered her eyelashes and played with the red curls that bounced around her rouged cheeks.

"Uh, yeah."

Banes poured sparingly. Holding the glass out to Annie, he tried to disguise the trembling.

"Harley, ya nervous?" she asked, looking over the rim of the glass.

Engrossed, Banes stood by the window watching the street. "Annie, go down and send Sikes up here."

Annie pouted. "Oh, Harley!"

"Do as I say!" Banes said sharply.

Annie downed her drink, figuring it was the last one on Harley, and closed the door after her. Banes waited until the knock on the door.

"Come in."

Sikes, a drifter, was rawboned and skittish. The red-rimmed eyes moved continuously about the room. The hat drooped over a pockmarked face in need of a shave. Banes had engaged him in a few hands of low-stakes poker and didn't particularly like him. He disliked everybody he had met at the Westerner. Banes figured all of them had crossed the law somewhere back on the trail. Running with drifters was not to his liking. He was better than that. Soon he would make his presence known in Lodgepole and lift himself back to respectability. But first he would take care of Colter.

Banes shoved the bottle to Sikes. "Sikes, I want ya to do somethin' for me."

Sikes took Annie's glass and flicked his tongue over thick lips. His inscrutable eyes danced with anticipation.

The drifter grinned, filling the glass. "Anythin' ya say, Harley."

Banes was dubious of Sikes, but he was the best available.

Banes said, "When ya see me leave, wait ten minutes, then go git Marshal Colter and tell him there's a fight at the Westerner, and that he better come quick before somebody git's killed. Ya got that?"

Sikes nodded vigorously. "Yeah, Harley, wait ten minutes, then go git Colter." He paused with a blank face, then asked, "How do I tell when ten minutes is up?"

Annoyed, Banes asked, "Ain't there a clock downstairs?"

Sikes took a drink and smacked his lips. "Ain't see'd one if there is."

"Here, take my watch." Banes reached into a pocket, brought out a watch, and added, "You know how to tell time?"

Sikes grinned over the rim of his glass. "Shore do, Harley. My mammy learnt me how."

"Okay, Sikes, I'm countin' on ya. Ten minutes after ya see me leave."

Banes flipped a gold coin to Sikes. "Take the bottle too. Now, leave me alone. I got some thinkin' to do."

Sikes grabbed the bottle and held it close. "Thanks, Harley, I won't fergit this."

Banes watched Sikes leave and felt a twinge of pity for men like him. He figured they were content with the crumbs of life. Banes peeked through the window curtain. A vague smile tugged at his mouth. His belly roiled at the prospect of getting Colter.

He lit the lamp and poured water into a bowl. Banes splashed his face and scrubbed it with a soiled towel. He grabbed a flat-crowned hat and adjusted it to slope down over his forehead and to the right. After buckling his gunbelt, he checked the Navy Colt and jammed it into the holster. Another peek through the curtain told him it was time to go. He crossed the room and softly closed the door behind him. Soon dusk would yield to darkness, signaling the start of a new life.

Chapter Sixteen

Sam forked the last bit of hay and left the mules munching contentedly. Pictures of the men he had seen earlier rolled through his mind. *Jed Colter, or was it Jedidiah?* The redheaded one, he had seen him before with the other three men. *Gibbs? Gibron? Gibbons! The redheaded one is Gibbons!* The tinkle of a bottle followed by a curse from the rear of the livery stopped Sam. Peeping through a crack in the wall, he saw the silhouette of a man. Darkness veiled the approaching figure until he stepped into the dim torchlight from Main Street. The man glanced toward Main and continued on his way behind the livery. *It was the man from the railroad! Bean? Banes!*

Sam quietly slipped out the back door. He paused, watching Banes. Where was he going? And why was he taking the back way? Longley called for him. Sam followed Banes, hugging the wall of each building. Banes stopped behind Vick's Merchantile Store, peered around the corner, then pulled back quickly. He eased a gun from his holster and waited. A dog barked in the distance and a child cried. He

157

shuddered from the night chill. Then he remembered. *Hackett! Where is Hackett? Banes is here, so Hackett can't be far away.* Sam's brow creased in thought. The three men with Gibbons and Colter. *They were Acker, Cain, and Trendell!* Gibbons had been captured, and they were free! He fingered the watch, remembering the initials JC engraved elegantly on the front. Thoughts inundated his mind like swarming bees. The green carpeted hills and valleys, distant mountains shrouded in a blue haze, the woman's picture in the watch, Colonel Mosby, Point Lookout. *Colter!*

"James Colter," he whispered. Exhilaration washed over him. *He was free!*

Banes looked over his shoulder and then stepped around the corner. Jim Colter gathered his wits and realized Banes was going to ambush somebody. He moved swiftly to the corner where Banes had stood. Clouds obscured the moon, plunging the alley into murkiness. He peeked around the corner and saw the shadowy Banes inching forward. Footsteps pounded on the boardwalk, then a figure passed by the alley entrance.

Soon, Jim Colter heard, "Marshal! Marshal Colter! Ya better come quick! There's a fight at the Westerner's! Somebody's gonna git kilt if ya don't hurry!"

Colter? Jed Colter? Jedidiah? That's Jedidiah! Is Banes after Jedidiah? Jim Colter froze. Fear gripped his chest as he moved stealthily to the opposite side of the alley and then eased forward. Banes thumbed back the hammer. The man he'd heard calling for the marshal ran by the alley. His boots hit the boardwalk and faded in the distance.

A door opened as Jim Colter closed the distance to Banes. Heavy boots on the boardwalk caught his ear, and then a tall figure stepped off the boardwalk. Jim gathered his strength and lunged forward.

"Jedidiah!"

Jed Colter heard the rustle from the alley, then his name, and suddenly a figure hurtled in front of him. Ear-splitting gunfire erupted and echoed down the alley. Colter instinctively dove to his left and grabbed his Colt. Again an orange dagger pierced the night. Hot lead creased his left arm. Colter's .44 belched fire, followed by a scream from Ma's. He fired again, then a wraithlike figure stumbled from the darkness and slumped forward, face-down.

Numbed, Jed Colter moved cautiously to the still body and turned it over with the toe of his boot. *Banes.* Somebody had called his name. *Jedidiah.* Colter's heart pounded. Only two people had ever called him Jedidiah: Ellen and his father. Quickly crossing the ally, he knelt by a crumpled body, oblivious to the gathering crowd. The whiskered, gaunt face was like a shadow in the dim light. Ellen gasped as she knelt by him.

"It's . . . it's Sam. Somebody get Doc," Ellen pleaded and cradled Jim Colter's head in her hands.

Baffled, Jed looked up. "Sam?"

Searching for words, she said, "Yes, he works for Asa."

Leaning over, Raisin' Cain drawled, "Miss Ellen, that ain't Sam. That's Cap'n Colter. Jed, that's your pa!"

Stunned, Jed gathered his father to his chest. Jim Colter groaned and opened his eyes.

Jed swallowed hard. "Pa, it's Jed."

Jim Colter's weary eyes looked up. "Jedidiah. Is it really you?"

"Yes, Pa," Jed replied around the lump in his throat.

Jim Colter's eyes closed, a tear trickled down his cheek, and then he slumped.

"Pa? Pa!" Jed said fearfully.

Pervasive thoughts of losing his father again suffocated him.

"Folks, move back, please," Doc Burke appealed.

Burke stopped short when he saw Jed Colter holding the body of a disheveled misfit. He had seen the man with Longley, but he didn't know his name.

"Jed," Burke said apprehensively. When he didn't get a response, Burke placed his hand on Colter's shoulder and said, "Let's get him over to my office."

Jed grimaced. "It's been so long, Doc, and now this. I can't believe it!"

Doc's brow creased in thought, wondering what Jed was taking about. At the moment, he would not ask.

Gently tugging at Jed's arm, Burke said urgently, "Come on, Jed. We must get him to my office."

Jed Colter nodded, then lifted his father and headed for Burke's office. He recalled the last time he saw his father: a robust man near two hundred pounds. Now, his frail body was mostly skin and bone.

Jed placed his father on the table. Blood was spreading across his chest. Ellen held a lamp nearby. Burke cut away the shirt, revealing a wound high on the left side of his chest. Burke searched for a heartbeat. Cain, Acker, and Trendell watched anxiously through the window.

"Heart's strong," Burke said, then added, "Let's take a closer look at that wound."

Doc pushed up his glasses, gently raised the left shoulder, and inspected the wound. Looking up, he said, "Clean wound. Went right through. He'll be out a while. Obviously, he's not in good physical condition."

Jed asked hopefully, "Doc, you mean he's going to be all right?"

"I believe so, but we've got a lot of work to do, with his condition being what it is."

Jed's smile stripped away the despair as he took his father's hand. Burke was perplexed by Jed's affection for this man.

"Jed, if you don't mind me asking, just who is he?"

"My father," Jed whispered shakily.

"Your father! How did . . . ?" Burke's questioning stare broke, then he continued, "I'll take care of your father. Miss Ellen, check Jed's wound."

Ellen looked up at Colter. "Jed, when is it going to end?"

"Soon as I get Draik and Hackett."

"Can't the cavalry do that? Why does it have to be you?"

"It's a civilian matter. Maybe it won't be me, but somebody will get Draik and Hackett."

Silently Jed Colter vowed he would not stop until he found them. He turned to hide his misty eyes.

Ellen's soft touch on his arm brought Jed around. He reached out and slowly pulled her to him. She yielded willingly and buried her head in his chest.

A Texas drawl broke the silence. "It's 'bout time you two did somethin'. Ya been lookin' like two roosters a waitin' to see who would make the first move."

Colter looked over his shoulder at the pallid Radison leaning against a door. A quirly hung precariously from his canted smile.

"Jed, remember what I told ya that night out on Lodgepole Creek?" Radison chuckled weakly, then winced before adding, "I'd say ya done got hawgtied."

Ellen brushed away a tear and looked up at Colter. "What's he talking about?"

Colter grinned sheepishly. "I'll tell you someday."

While Ellen cleaned and bandaged his wound, Jed

Colter's mind wandered. He thought of the many places he had looked for his father and reflected on how incredible it was to find him in Lodgepole. His mother had never lost hope. Jed smiled, thinking of Micah and Ruth.

"Why are you smiling?" Ellen asked.

"I was thinking about Micah and Ruth and my mother. I've got to let them know." Jed grew pensive, then added, "I hope Pa will be all right."

"He'll be fine," Ellen reassured him.

Jed closed his eyes, took a deep breath, and slowly exhaled. The tension and disappointments of the past two years drained from his body. When Ellen finished dressing his wound, Jed remembered, "I've got some business at the Westerner's Saloon."

Cain, Acker, and Trendell converged on Colter as he left Burke's office.

"How is Captain Colter?" Acker asked.

Jed's grin was answer enough, but then he said, "He's going to be all right."

They whooped and vigorously shook his hand.

"Jed, don't worry 'bout Cap'n Colter," Cain said, then nodded at Acker and Trendell. "Me, Buck, and Matt'll look after him."

"Thanks, men. It'll mean a lot to him knowing you are here."

Jed Colter approached the Westerner's thinking about the man who had told him about the fight at the saloon. He figured Banes had hired the man to set him up for an ambush.

The Westerner's Saloon seemed peaceful enough as Colter stepped through the front door. The saloon was small, having only four tables. Hicks, the bartender, leaned his elbows on the bar, eyeing Colter. A lantern at each end of the bar provided light, and a stairway at the rear of the saloon led upstairs. Colter's gaze swung around the saloon. Four shaggy men were engaged in a card game at one of the tables. Abruptly, laughter broke off. The odor of stale sweat and sour whiskey hung in the air along with the gray haze of smoke.

"Any trouble tonight?" Colter asked Hicks.

Hicks' beefy jowls shook like jelly when he said, "None, Marshal. You must've had some up the street. What happened?"

"Banes tried to ambush me. Did you see anybody leave here and then come back?"

"Banes ambushed ya?" Hicks shook his head and went on, "Never woulda figgered that. Was a likeable fella. Banes left and then that fella, Sikes, left 'bout ten minutes later. Then Sikes, he comes back, all out of breath. I take it Banes is dead?"

Colter nodded. "Sikes here?"

With a lift of his eyes, Hicks said, "Upstairs in one of the rooms, probably with Annie."

Colter glanced at the card players. Two he had seen before, the others he had not. He checked his .44, replaced the two spent cartridges, then eased up the stairs. After positioning himself outside a door, Colter called out, "Sikes!"

A chafed voice said, "Yeah, what'cha want?"

Colter stepped back and kicked the door open. Annie shrieked, and Sikes paled at the sight of Colter's leveled gun.

"Surprised to see me, Sikes?"

The acerbic Sikes asked, "What'cha mean, Marshal?"

Colter snapped, "You know what I mean. Banes hired you to set me up for an ambush. Come on, you're going to jail."

Sikes argued, "Marshal, I didn't know Banes wuz gonna ambush ya. He told me to come git ya ten minutes after he left here. I'd no sooner got back than I heard them shots. Is he dead?"

"You'll be, too, if you don't get moving."

Sikes looked askance at Annie and left the room with Colter. Sikes, in his own way, was telling the truth. After a few days in jail, Colter would tell him to move on.

Colter shoved Sikes into a cell next to Gibbons and then stepped outside. He slipped into the shadows by the jail and paused. Uncertainty tugged at him. Banes had unobtrusively slipped into Lodgepole and tried to kill him. Where were Draik and Hackett? Draik's ego wouldn't allow him to backshoot anyone. He had a reputation to build. Hackett? Hackett would kill any way he could. Colter's eyes moved from Ma's, to Vick's, the livery, the bank, the Westerner's, then to Burke's office. He detected no suspicious movement. One of Kilbane's men lounged in front of Vick's. Colter kept to the shadows and paused at each alley until he got to Burke's.

Heads swiveled when Colter stepped into Burke's office. Doc rested his head on the desk while Ellen and Longley sat by Jim Colter's bed in the next room.

Longley said, "Jed, Miss Ellen and me wanted to tell ya 'bout your pa, but we wuzn't sure it wuz him."

"How did you know?" Colter asked.

"The eyes," Longley replied.

"And the voice," Ellen added.

"Doc, how long will he be unconscious?"

Burke shrugged. "Hard to say. In his condition, could be today, maybe tomorrow."

Colter said, "I don't understand. Why didn't he come forward before now?"

Burke removed his glasses. A frown wrinkled his brow.

"My guess is your father suffered a temporary loss of

memory from the beatings, and now he's recovered enough to recognize people he knew. My only concern is his physical condition. Soon as he wakes, we'll start feeding him to get his strength back." Burke turned to his desk. "Jed, I found this in his pocket."

Colter felt Ellen at his side as he examined the watch and fingered the initials . . . JC. He opened the cover. The picture of his mother, yellowed with age, looked softly at him.

"She's beautiful. Your mother?"

"Yes."

Colter opened the envelope and read the letter, as much as he could. He recognized his mother's handwriting. His eyes strayed to the shoes under the table. What remained were paper-thin soles attached to ragged tops by leather thongs. Ankle shackles had left ugly scars. A length of rope held up baggy pants. Wicked scars from Hackett's whip crisscrossed his torso. He had never hated anyone, but Colter's hatred for Hackett smoldered.

"Jed, just like Jesus, he took them stripes for us," Cain said tremulously. "Hackett's an animal. Thar's not a kind thought in him. I don't know what makes a man like that."

"I'd be dead now if he hadn't taken that bullet," Colter said.

"That's the Cap'n's way," Cain grinned, then added, " 'Stead of you saving his life, he saved yore's."

Ellen took Colter by the arm. "Jed, all of you need rest. I'll stay with your father and send for you if there's any change. I'll have fresh clothes for you men in the morning."

Colter felt Ellen's soft hand in his as she herded them to the door.

Outside, Colter lingered while the men went ahead. Ellen stood in the doorway. Her face was soft and beautiful in the lamplight. She waited eagerly as Colter cupped her face between his hands and tilted her head. She warmly accepted his gentle kiss. Colter thought no moment could be sweeter than this. Ellen filled the void in his life. He had found his father and the other men. Suddenly, the euphoria was tempered by the thought of unfinished business.

Ellen pressed her cheek against Colter's chest. Reaching up, her lips touched his ear and whispered, "You need a shave."

With a coy smile, she slipped out of his arms and returned to Burke's office. The ghost of David Easton was slipping away. Colter smiled, turned on a heel, and headed for Ma's. The aroma of food stoked his appetite. Ma's mischievous smile met him at the door. He wondered what she was thinking. She had been acting strange ever since Ellen had arrived.

Ma gathered the apron in her hands. "Come in, Jed. I've got a plate ready."

"Thanks, Ma." Colter sniffed. "It smells good."

Ma could see Burke's office from the window, and what she had seen tonight pleased her. Things were moving faster than she had hoped.

Colter asked, "Where are the men?"

"Upstairs, probably sleeping by now. They sure are a tuckered-out bunch."

"First roof they've had over their heads in two years," Colter said pensively.

"Got some bath water ready."

Colter looked up at Ma and smiled. "You must have read my mind. Now that scares me."

Colter cleaned his plate, pushed back his chair, and trudged upstairs. After bathing, he slept, unaware of two men who had slipped down the southern rim of the valley under cover of darkness.

Chapter Seventeen

Jed Colter awoke at dawn, refreshed. He lit the lamp, then shaved and dressed. After strapping on his gunbelt, he descended the stairs to find Acker, Cain, and Trendell busily chewing on steak and eggs. A look around told him Ellen wasn't there.

Ma read his thoughts. "She's over at Doc's, Jed."

Colter stepped outside and saw a dust cloud to the east. Even after years Colter recognized Bert Kilbane as he and his men drew even with the Westerner's Saloon. Kilbane smiled as they pulled alongside Colter.

"Jed, it's good to see you again," Kilbane beamed, clasping Colter's hand.

"Too long, Bert. What brings you over this way?"

Kilbane grinned, leaned forward, and whispered, "Mainly to see you. We've got a lot of catching up to do."

"That we do."

"I wish we had more time to visit, but we're overdue at Fort Russell. Any word on your father?"

Colter grinned. "You believe in miracles? I came out

167

here to find him, but as it turned out he found me. He saved me by taking a bullet meant for me."

"Then he's alive?"

Colter thumbed over his shoulder. "He's over at Doc Burke's. Doc thinks he'll be all right."

He told Kilbane of finding the prisoners, the bank robbery, and Radison being gunned down.

"I heard there was trouble over here, so I sent Quigley and Zeman over to help out. We're not supposed to stick our noses in civilian affairs, but since you were here I didn't think you would mind."

"I'm glad you did."

"We'll take them back with us."

"I have a prisoner by the name of Abe Gibbons. I'm certain he's a deserter. He was a sergeant in charge of guard detail at Point Lookout Prison Camp when my father was smuggled out."

"I'll check it out."

"One other piece of business. There was another prisoner by the name of Jake Lemmon. Gibbons and his partner killed him and dumped the body over on Plum Creek. There's probably not much left of him, but maybe enough to verify his death."

"Jed, we ain't leavin' 'til we know," Cain said as he and Acker joined them.

"We find Lemmon."

Colter turned to see Little Raven and Johnny Hawk.

The stern-faced Little Raven continued. "Find body on Plum Creek. The Cheyenne raidin' over there. Find clothes with letter. Bury body, take letter to Major North. He said letter to Sergeant Jake Lemmon."

Johnny Hawk grinned. "This Lemmon, he not tough like Sam."

"Sam?" Colter asked, remembering Ellen had called his father by that name.

Jed Colter listened with amazement as Johnny Hawk told of finding Sam on Lodgepole Creek and how Sam had killed the Arapaho brave.

"We take Sam to John Leach's ranch." Hawk grinned, then added, "Sam, he like John Colter."

Asa Longley joined them and heard Hawk's last words. Then he said, "Sam *is* Colter . . . Jim Colter. He's Marshal Colter's pa."

Johnny Hawk's mouth dropped. He glanced at Little Raven, smiled, and poked him with an elbow.

Colter said, "I don't know how to thank you."

Little Raven lifted his chin and said, "He call hisself Sam."

"Doc Burke said he probably lost his memory from all the beatings he took. My father couldn't remember his name, so he called himself Sam."

Colter turned to Cain and Acker. "What do you know about Lemmon?"

Acker said, "He rode with Mosby. Jake's from Virginia, near my family. I'll see that they are notified."

Colter nodded, then turned to Kilbane. "Bert, I'm going over to check on Pa. Got time to visit?"

"Not this time. Got some business at the bank, then we'll head back to Fort Russell."

"I told Quigley I would get him the information to send telegrams to my mother and the families of the prisoners."

"I'll see that they are sent. What about the future?" Kilbane asked. "I hear the Union Pacific has plans to establish a town west of the Black Hills. It'll be important to the railroad. I smell opportunity there."

"I've been reading law. Someday I'll practice. The opportunities are here, especially with the railroad coming."

Kilbane smiled. "And Miss Wellsley?"

Colter dropped his chin and grinned. Kilbane laughed and slapped Colter on the back.

"She's a beautiful lady, Jed. I wish the best to you and Ellen. Next time there's a dance at Fort Russell I would like for you and Ellen to come."

"I'd like that. Let me know, and we'll try to work it out. You know I'm not much at dancing."

Kilbane grinned. "I'm counting on that."

After Kilbane departed, Colter was surprised to find that Little Raven and Johnny Hawk had slipped away unnoticed. He hurriedly covered the distance to Burke's and eased through the door. Doc took notice of Ellen's shy smile and lingering look at Jed.

Burke nodded toward Jim Colter. "He's coming around. Rested well last night. How's that arm?"

"Fine, Doc."

Burke pushed out of his chair. "Let me change that bandage."

"I'll take care of it," Ellen said quickly, taking Colter by the arm. She added dourly, "You'll have to take off your shirt."

"Doc?" Colter nervously petitioned Burke.

"Better do as she says." Burke chuckled and busied himself at his desk.

Radison stuck his head around the corner. "Yeah, ya better do like Miss Ellen says," he said.

"It's not like I've never seen a man's body." Ellen glanced demurely up at Colter and smiled. Purposely, she let him stew before continuing. "I worked in a Confederate hospital during the war."

Ellen finished dressing Colter's wound and watched him gingerly slip on the shirt and stuff it inside his belt.

Weakly, Radison asked, "Doc, when ya gonna let me go?"

"You can go when you're ready." Burke paused and shook a finger at Radison. "Let me tell you something. Don't do anything crazy like going back on the job for a while. You've got a ways to go before you're healed. And I want to see you back in here so I can check you out."

Colter said, "I'm going to see Corporal Quigley."

"You mind some company?" Ellen asked.

She smiled, taking the arm Colter offered. Both were preoccupied. Ellen looked up at him. "Did you know that Luke was once married?"

"Luke? Married?"

"Luke had a wedding ring on when he was shot. I had never seen it before."

"Neither had I."

Ellen related what Radison had told Burke.

"I figured there was something in Luke's past. At times he gets gloomy."

"Luke's been carrying an awful burden." Spotting Kilbane's troops, she squeezed his arm. "What's the cavalry doing here?" she asked.

"Bert's got some business at the bank, then they are returning to Fort Russell."

"So, you saw him?"

"Yes."

They arrived at Ma's. Ellen said, "Thanks for the company." She looked over her shoulder and smiled radiantly, then disappeared into Ma's.

Colter recalled Radison's good-natured warning, "Better watch that filly. She'll rope and hawgtie ya."

Jed Colter had a sixth sense when trouble was near. His boots pounded the boardwalk, and then he crossed Main to the jail. Colter's eyes darted to each alley and rooftop. He was being watched and felt it.

"Mornin', Marshal," Quigley said.

"Corporal Quigley, how are things?"

"Quiet as a mouse."

"Captain Kilbane wants you and Zeman to go back to Fort Russell with him." Colter took a paper from his pocket and passed it to Quigley. "I need these telegrams sent. You'll find the names and where to send them on this paper," he added.

"Yes, sir."

"And one other thing. If there are any replies to those telegrams, have someone bring them over here."

"Yes, sir."

"Marshal, when ya gonna let me out?"

Sikes pressed his face between the cell bars.

Colter snapped, "I'm thinking about charging you with conspiracy to commit murder."

"Murder?" Sikes whined. "Now wait a minute, Marshal, I ain't done no such thang!"

Colter wanted Sikes to think about what he had done before running him out of Lodgepole. He figured if Sikes dwelled on it he would never again want to hear the name Lodgepole.

Turning to Quigley, Colter said, "Thanks, Corporal. You and Zeman better get moving. The captain's probably waiting."

While Colter had breakfast at Ma's, Kilbane and his troops filed past on their way to Fort Russell.

"Ma, where are the men?"

"They're upstairs taking baths. Ellen brought some clothes for them and a razor. They'll be like new when we see them again."

He heard a muffled voice, "Ma, we need more water up here."

"Coming right up!" Ma shouted.

Colter said, "I'll take it up."

"Thanks, Jed. I'm tuckered out from packing water up those stairs."

Colter ascended the stairs, hearing voices and laughter. After a knock, Acker cracked the door open and then swung it wide.

"Got your water," Colter said.

The men were clean-shaven. Cain was in the tub, scrubbing his fingernails. Damp towels littered the floor. Acker and Trendell had dressed in their new clothes.

Trendell smiled and said, "Jed, it's been a long time since I felt this good."

"This town got a barber?" Acker asked.

"Judson Vick at Vick's Merchantile, and tell him I'll settle up with him later."

Cain asked anxiously, "How's Cap'n Colter?"

"Doc says he's coming around."

Cain looked up at Colter. "Soon's we git through here, we'll sit with him. We ain't leavin' 'til he's up and about."

After a pause, Colter said, "Quigley and Zeman are returning to Fort Russell with Captain Kilbane. They'll be sending telegrams to your folks. Troops from Fort Russell will be coming in the next day or so to escort you to Cheyenne and see that you get to the end of track to catch a train home."

Cain whooped and splashed water over the sides of the tub. Acker and Trendell laughed. Colter felt close to these men, maybe because of his father. They were tough and hardened to the realities of life.

Colter left them and moved briskly down the stairs. He

paused on the boardwalk and drew in the sweet high plains air. His gaze moved along Main, then up to Vick's rooftop. The sky hugged the horizon. Colter was angling toward Burke's office when he heard uneven footsteps on the boardwalk. A chalkfaced Asa Longley approached.

"What's wrong, Asa?"

Asa pointed a shakey finger toward the Westerner's Saloon. "J-Jed, that's him."

"Who?"

"Th-that ugly snake fella that gunned down Sheriff Radison."

Colter's eyes swung to the slender figure moving slowly, inexorably toward him. Even at this distance, he recognized Shad Draik. Colter flexed his fingers, lifted his .44 and eased it back in the holster. He recalled the time in Sedalia when Draik went into a rage after a man had called him Snake.

"Asa, go on over to Doc's and stay there." When Longley lingered, Colter snapped, "Hurry!"

Longley grabbed his right leg and scurried to Burke's office.

Colter's eyes fixed on Draik as he angled to the center of Main. The distance closed, then Draik stopped and spread his feet. Deliberately, he raised a hand, removed the quirly from his mouth, and tossed it aside. His gaze held on Colter as he blew smoke from his lungs. Judson Vick retreated to a doorway. Drifters from the Westerner's Saloon spilled out into the street, taking bets. The distant call of a quail pierced the stillness of the valley. The plains wind was eerily motionless. A mongrel dog trotted down an alley sniffing for food.

"Howdy, Marshal."

Colter moved measuredly. His eyes fell hard on Draik as

his right hand curled near the .44. Draik rocked back on his heels, and then steadied himself. The droopy eyes peered from under the hat brim and narrowed when Colter stopped.

Colter's square jaw corded, then he admonished, "Draik, I see the lesson in Sedalia didn't take."

Draik's mouth lifted in a sloped smile. "I learnt a lot, Colter, and now I'm gonna teach *you* a thing or two."

Colter's eyes drifted to Draik's gun. This time there was something different about the young gunfighter. He was deadly and cocksure. Colter remembered Red Ilson's warning, "He's older and wiser."

Colter raised his chin and said calmly, "I'm waiting, Draik."

Draik threw back his head and laughed, but there was emptiness in the gunfighter's laughter.

"Colter, I'm a lucky man, but your luck's run out. That sheriff drew iron on me. I kilt him and now I'm gonna take ya down."

"You didn't kill Sheriff Radison. You shot him up good, but he's too tough to die."

Draik's smile transmuted to a twisted sneer. "You're lyin,' Colter! I put three bullets in him. He weren't even breathin'. I been trackin' that sheriff. He hung two of my brothers down in Texas. Didn't even give 'em a chance."

"From what I hear they got what was coming to them. Any man who would do what they did to Radison's wife deserves hanging. I would've done the same."

Colter sensed Draik was losing his edge.

Draik flexed his fingers. "Understand you're lookin' for Hackett. He's right here in Lodgepole. Hired me to kill ya. Too bad ya won't git the chance to meet him, 'cept in hell." Draik laughed.

Colter chided, "Draik, you talk too much. Hackett's sent

a boy to do his work. Unless you're afraid of cashing in, fill your hand, Snake."

Draik's face grew crimson, then his right shoulder flinched. He had not cleared leather when Colter brought up his gun in a fluid motion. Draik's jaw dropped and his eyes flared in disbelief as Colter's .44 bucked and roared. A death knell reverberated through Lodgepole and up the slopes of the valley.

Seemingly, Draik was suspended on tiptoe with a blank stare and a widening splotch of red on his chest. The gun slipped from his fingers, and then he pitched forward into the dust. Colter emptied the spent cartridge and shoved in another.

The somber undertaker ambled over, sizing up the body.

Colter said, "Don't move him until I say so. Looks like it's going to be a good day for you."

"No disrespect to the dead, but I could use a good day. I'll just take a peek to see what kind of box I need to fit 'im in."

The marshal nodded and rested his gaze on the Westerner's Saloon.

Chapter Eighteen

Pug Hackett's massive hulk stepped through the batwing doors of the saloon. A bullwhacker's whip trailed over his right shoulder. Acker and Trendell hit the boardwalk running. They paused to look at Draik and stopped at the sight of Hackett. Cain joined them, struggling to button his shirt.

Hackett eyed Draik's body disdainfully. He had counted on the gunman taking Colter, but Draik was no match for the marshal. Hackett couldn't match Colter's gun either. His fists were his only chance. Colter, with an easy, confident walk, neared the range of Hackett's whip. The bullwhacker unbuckled his gunbelt and threw it to a saloon drifter, figuring Colter wouldn't shoot an unarmed man.

Hackett spit, dimpling the dust. "Well, Colter, I reckon it's 'tween you and me now."

"You reckon right," Colter said tight-lipped.

"I figger ya to be a tough one. Thought we got'cha back at Lodgepole Crick. Let's see how tough ya really are. How 'bout settlin' this with fists?"

Colter smiled. "I like the idea, Hackett."

"Colter, ya oughta know," Hackett paused and gloated, "nobody's ever took me."

"Nobody's ever took me either."

Colter untied the leather thong above his knee, then unbuckled the gunbelt and tossed it to Cain.

Cain warned, "Jed, Hackett carries a knife in his right boot."

"Well now, Cain, ain't ya lookin' fit," Hackett jeered. "Soon's I git through with Colter here, I'll take care o' you three."

"Hackett, you need that whip?" Colter goaded. "Your fists not enough?"

Hackett laughed and abruptly brought the whip over his shoulder, issuing a loud crack by Colter's left ear. Colter was taken aback by the quickness of the big man. He had to get closer to offset the leverage Hackett needed. Hackett brought the whip back to deliver the stinging blow. Colter timed his move and bolted quickly. He closed the distance to Hackett, making the whip ineffective. Hackett's huge girth and short, powerful arms were intimidating. Colter distanced himself from those arms. The bullwhacker's beady eyes gleamed in anticipation.

Hackett tossed the whip aside, then he and Colter circled like fighting roosters. Colter crouched to add leverage to his punches. He ducked, bobbed, weaved, and stayed on the move. Colter drew on the boxing skills he had learned at West Point. He stuck a stiff jab to Hackett's nose and then another, followed up with a right to the belly. Colter danced away and to the rear of Hackett. As Hackett turned, Colter caught him flush on the jaw, dug a left to the belly, and shuffled out of reach. Frustration began to build in Hackett as Cain, Acker, and Trendell shouted encouragement.

"Colter, if I wanted to dance I'd a brung a woman. Stand still and fight like a man!"

Hackett charged, groping with his short arms. Colter nimbly moved to the right and hooked a short left to the mouth, splitting Hackett's lip. Blood spilled down his chin and doubt wiggled into Hackett's eyes. Hackett rushed at Colter like a wild bull, flailing away with little damage. Colter winced when a sledgehammer blow found his belly. Quickly, he twisted out of danger. Colter measured Hackett, planted his feet, and swung with both fists to the face before switching to the belly. Tiring, Hackett lost his wind. Hackett lunged in desperation. His right arm encircled Colter's waist. Colter clubbed at Hackett's head and wrenched free. Hackett fell to his knees and glared at Colter from glazed, hate-filled eyes. He wobbled, gasping for air, then reached for the knife. Colter expected the move and sent Hackett headlong into the dust with a brutal right. The knife fell from Hackett's hand. Colter kicked it over to Cain.

Dazed, Hackett struggled to his hands and knees. He leered at Colter from a mask of blood and dust, then shook his massive head to clear the cobwebs. Colter backed away and motioned to Cain for his gunbelt.

"Look out, Jed, he's got a gun!" Cain shouted, then tossed the gunbelt to Colter.

Colter spun around as Hackett fired. The bullet fanned a breeze by his ear. Colter leveled the .44 and felt its kick against his palm. Hackett fell back, clutching his gutshot belly. A lingering, torturous death awaited Hackett.

"Colter!" Hackett screamed. "Kill me, Colter! Don't let me die like this!"

Colter's eyes swung around the crowd as he approached Hackett. He looked down at the bullwhacker. "Hackett, you're going to feel every lash of the whip you laid on these men. You're going to feel every beating you gave them. You're an animal. You deserve to die." Colter turned and said, "Matt, get Doc."

Burke came on the run and knelt by Hackett. He shook his head, looked up at Colter, and said, "Nothing I can do for him. Maybe some laudanum for his pain, but that won't help much. Let's get him over to the office."

Cain, Acker, and Trendell pulled and tugged at Hackett while he cursed and screamed. Hackett refused to be put on the table. He lay on the floor writhing and cursing. Sweat trickled copiously down his blood-crusted face.

Burke said, "Hackett, let me give you something for the pain."

Hackett's lips curled in a sneer. "I don't need no help! I'm gonna die like a man!"

Cain, Acker, and Trendell stood vigil. Kneeling by Hackett, Cain said, "Guess you're the loser after all, Hackett. Cap'n Colter's in the next room. I wish he could see ya."

Hackett glared at Cain, took a deep breath, and then his eyes grew wide. His face contorted in horror as life ebbed and ended with a vacant, distant stare.

While Burke attended to Hackett, Jed Colter stood silently in the street, reflecting on what had happened. Suddenly, he felt alone. Taking a life was not his way, but sometimes there was no other choice. He heard running feet on the boardwalk and looked up as Ellen rushed into his arms.

"It's over, Ellen," Colter whispered, and held her close.

"Jed! Your father is awake!" Burke shouted from his office door.

Colter and Ellen hurried their pace to Burke's office. Jed glanced at Hackett's lifeless body. Jim Colter was sitting on a cot. Jed sat by his father and gently put an arm around his shoulders. Doc and Ellen waited in the next room with Cain, Acker, and Trendell.

"Pa, you're going to be all right. You saved my life."

"Jedidiah . . . ," Jim Colter said, then paused to gather himself. A tear trickled into his beard. He took a deep breath and winced. Surveying his condition, Jim laughed softly. "I'm not much to look at, am I?"

"Pa, you never looked better."

"I saw the men. Where are they?" Jim asked.

Cain approached. "Right here, Cap'n Colter. Matt and Buck are here too."

Acker and Trendell ambled in and stood by Cain, followed by Doc and Ellen.

"You men all right?"

Cain said, "Yes, sir, after we got some grub in us and some new clothes."

"I heard somebody scream, or did I imagine that?"

Cain grinned. "That was Hackett, Cap'n, when he saw the gates of hell."

Jim Colter looked up at Cain and asked, "Hackett's dead?"

Cain nodded. "Jed took care of Hackett."

"And Gibbons is in jail," Jed added.

Jim Colter fingered his beard and then his hair. He looked around at each face.

Ellen knelt by Jed and took his hand. Jed said shyly, "Pa, this is Ellen Wellsley."

Jim Colter's eyes twinkled, looking inquisitively from Ellen to Jed.

"We'll fill you in on all the details later, Mr. Colter." Ellen smiled and softly touched him on the shoulder. "Right now, I'll get you something to eat."

Suddenly, Jim grabbed Jed's arm. "Sarah!"

"I've sent for Mother, Micah, and Ruth. Soon as you get something to eat, I want you to rest. We've got plenty of time to catch up. I've got to take care of some business."

The marshal checked Hackett's pockets and came up with several coins. He found no money belt.

"Raisin', would you go down to the saloon and bring up Draik's horse? He's a dun. Buck, see if you can round up Hacket's horse. The saloon would be a good place to start."

"Yes, sir," they answered in unison.

Meanwhile, Colter went to Draik and checked the gunman's pockets. Several double eagle gold coins rolled out onto the ground.

"Guess that would be the bank's money. What about a money belt? Uh huh, there it is, and fat."

Cain brought up the dun. Colter went through the saddlebags and pulled out two sacks containing money.

"At least we'll get some of it back."

A shaggy chestnut trailed Trendell. "Here he is, Jed. Not much to look at. Reminds me of its owner."

Colter patiently went through the saddlebags and found nothing of value.

"Men, take those horses over to Asa at the livery. And check those saddles good to make sure there is nothing hidden away. I'm going to take this money over to the bank."

Colter entered the bank and went to the lone teller's window.

The teller said, "Marshal, you got a big deposit there."

"It's the bank's money. Recovered this from the bank robber."

Reaching into a pocket, he pulled out the coins he had

found on Hackett and Draik and placed them alongside the moneysacks.

"Marshal, I can't thank you enough."

"Just curious, how much did he take?"

"We just sorted out all of that. It was three thousand two hundred and twenty-nine dollars even."

"I don't know how much we got back, but if there is more there than was taken, would you see that Mrs. Nenquist gets it?"

"Of course, Marshal. That poor lady is taking it real hard. I try to do what I can for her."

Cain and Trendell burst through the door. Trendell said, "Jed, we found this pouch Draik had sewed under his saddle. Looks like money in there. Didn't find nothing on Hackett's saddle."

Colter handed the pouch to the teller.

"This is much better than I expected, Marshal. Tell you the truth, I didn't expect anything. We will count it and maybe there'll be enough that Mrs. Nenquist will get some."

"Men, we better go so he can count the money."

The teller stuck his hand through the teller cage window. "Again, Marshal, thank you."

Three days later, Jim Colter joined Jed and Ellen at Ma's. Doc Burke marveled at Jim's recovery. A new pair of shoes, fresh clothes, and a shave and haircut had transformed him. Ellen saw the square Colter jaw and the handsome features. His smile was like Jed's, broad and accenting his chin. The walk was confident and more upright than before.

"Jedidiah, I've been thinking. Virginia and the South are in for some hard times. There's something about this wild country that's appealing to me. A man could take some cattle and graze them in the high meadows. And with the railroad providing a ready market, a fella could do right well."

Jed looked at his father. "You getting at something, Pa?"

Cain, Acker, and Trendell joined them.

"I'm thinking of selling the farm in Virginia and moving out here."

Jed was taken aback. Before he could answer, Cain said, "Cap'n, I don't know 'bout Matt and Buck, but I'd like to join ya. That is, if you'd want me to."

Acker nodded, "Count me in, Captain Colter."

"Me, too," Buck Trendell joined in.

Jim Colter looked around the table. "I want you men to go back home and see your families before you make any commitments. Agreed?"

All nodded, then Cain said, "Agreed."

The more he thought about it, the more Jed Colter liked what he was hearing. What would his mother think? Leaving the green hills and mountains of Virginia would be difficult.

Boots on the boardwalk caught Jed's ear, then Radison eased through the door, followed by Corporal Quigley.

Reaching into a pocket, Quigley said, "Marshal Colter, got some telegrams here."

Jed fingered through the telegrams and passed one to Acker, then to Trendell and Cain. He read the one from his mother, and then passed it to his father.

After reading the telegram, Jim's chin quivered slightly. He asked, "How long will it take them to get here?"

Jed said, "By the time they get themselves together, maybe two weeks."

Jim Colter looked at Cain, Acker, and Trendell. "Men, I trust you heard from your families?"

They were pensive, and then broke into wide smiles.

"Yes, sir," Cain said. He added, "We're gonna miss ya Cap'n, but we'll be back."

Jed looked up at Quigley. "Corporal, see about getting an escort over to Cheyenne for these men and to the end of track."

"Yes, sir. Captain Kilbane said to tell you that Gibbons is a deserter. He'll be sending over an escort to take Gibbons to Fort Russell."

Jed Colter stood and offered a hand. "Thank you for what you and Private Zeman have done here. Give my regards to the captain."

"Yes, sir, I will."

"Let's celebrate," Jed said. "Ma, you have an apple pie back there?"

Ma peeked out the kitchen door. Ellen smiled as she disappeared into the kitchen, then reappeared with an apple pie and fresh coffee.

"Here you are, gentlemen."

Jim Colter said, "Sheriff Radison, I understand you've done some ranching."

Radison fingered his mustache and nodded, contemplating.

Jim continued, "How would you like to be my ramrod?"

"Where at? In Virginia?" Radison drawled.

"No. Right here in Wyoming."

Radison thought a moment, then a crooked smile crossed his face. "I'd like that, Mr. Colter."

Jed said, "I could handle any legal work, Pa."

Surprised, Jim asked, "You?"

"I've been reading law. It's time I used some of that knowledge. I know a lawyer in Cheyenne who will help."

Ellen took in the conversation as she refreshed their coffee.

"Well, now," Jim said, rubbing a hand along his jaw. "Luke, we better start planning that ranch and what kind of house to build." He paused, looked up at Ellen, then continued, "We need a nice place for our grandchildren to visit, maybe even live there."

Ellen beamed and timidly glanced at Jed. Squirming, Jed grinned sheepishly and pulled the hat low to hide his crimson face.

Peace had returned to Lodgepole. The bank teller had told Jed the day before that the amount of money recovered exceeded the amount taken by one hundred and fifteen dollars. Jed thought of a life with Ellen. The way he figured it, the future couldn't look any better.